THE

FORBIDDEN

PATH

THE FORBIDDEN PATH

SBPC

SIMMS BOOKS PUBLISHING CORPORATION

SBPC

SIMMS BOOKS PUBLISHING CORP.

Publishers Since 2012

Published by Simms Books Publishing Corporation

Jonesboro, GA

Library of Congress Cataloging in Publication Data

2018950144

Kingdawud Mujahid Burgess

THE FORBIDDEN PATH

ISBN: 978-09983311-9-5

Printed in the United States of America

Book Arrangement by Simms Books Publishing

Editor Mary Hoekstra

Cover by Urias Brown

DEDICATION

Do you think just because you say you believe that you will not be tested?

Shout out to my baby girl and life time friend Shanita Miller who gave up Christianity to become Muslim which was a very difficult transition. We are engaged to get married and I hope to bring you joy for the rest of your life if you let me. Stay close to me. loving someone is easy but loving someone when it's the hardest thing to do defines true love. everyone shall have that which they strive for so if you sincere strive for us to be together then you may have a life with me. Patience is rewarded 100 times fold.

To me you have been a bright light in a very dark place. Continue to be that and let nothing or no one pull you away from me and I will remain in your heart and mind forever.

As-salamu Alaykum Tawheed. hopefully everything is going well with you.

As-salamu Alaykum Jamal and jihad Timothy Smith who taught me a lot about patience. As-salamu Alaykum Isha Mael and Mustapha who are two of the youngest brothers and wisest I met in jail.

As-salamu Alaykum to the Mahdi family surely your father blessed this world by Allah's will with you brothers and sisters.

As-salamu Alaykum to my beautiful wife Najla Saleem al Asmi and I send my salaams to the entire Al Asmi family in Oman.

As-salamu Alaykum to Iman Aziz and Hanif Aziz, you both have had a huge impact on my thoughts when writing this book. As-salamu Alaykum to Sifee from Palestine and the brothers from Yemen who were incarcerated with me in Winton, N.C.

As-salamu Alaykum to Aza Furhan you are and will always be very special to me. As-salamu Alaykum Karima Fode, Atika Zeroul, Muna Samatar, Tasleem, and so many others. As-salamu Alaykum to everyone whose story has also contributed to this book such as Iman Ali Tamimi. Your story is a huge inspiration to this world.

As-salamu Alaykum to all of the brothers incarcerated such as Muq Sin, Mubashir, Dawud, Nazeem, Abdul Aziz, Habir, Lateef, Bamba Saine, Tay, Lamont L, stay on your deen Ahki.

16 years and 8 months incarcerated has given me the chance to study and learn about my lord, my prophet and the way of life called Islam. I have not wasted a second of my time in prison writing over 37 novels, 5,000 poems, completing many trade classes and college courses and keeping my body and mind in great shape.

Without having gone to prison I know I would not have found time to write one of these books, so Alhamdulillah! All praises be to Allah for the good and what we perceive is bad surely it may really be a good thing.

This life simple prepares us for the next to come. I have prepared myself by staying away from that which is forbidden and it was Allah's mercy that kept me away from most of it by keeping me restrained by the walls and gates of prison.

I have a lot more to offer the world that when I came in this place and I can't wait to share all of my life's experiences with the world. Thanks to my father who first introduced me to Islam or what he perceived to be Islam. May Allah guide you and rectify your affairs.

Chapter 1

After running down six flights of stairs, Faris was out of breath. He bent over at the waist, with his hands on his knees and yelled,

"Doctor Tamimi, please stop."

Doctor Tamimi, who was about to walk out the door, stopped in his tracks, then turned to face his favorite student.

"And what is so important that you had to catch me in person, instead of just having the school contact me," the doctor asked, as he made his way back to where Faris had slumped over.

Faris, still trying to catch his breath, looked up at his professor and smiled.

"I and many of your other students have been debating the subject of fasting. We all are fasting this week and some of us are fasting for religious reasons, as well as for health reasons.

Faris, regaining his breath said,

"Sarah has stated that those of us who are not fasting strictly for the sake of Our Lord will have no reward for the fast we have endured, which does not at all sound true. We needed to know if what she said is true, and if not, then what are the conditions of a person fasting for the sake of their Lord, as well as fasting to lose weight, all in one?"

Doctor Tamimi smiled, then removed his glasses and stared into Faris' eyes. After placing his reading glasses atop his head, he cleared his throat. He began,

"Our pious predecessors are all in agreement that if a person does any good deed, in order for it to be accepted by Allah, it has to be done strictly for his sake in the manner our beloved prophet had done a thing.

"You will find the proof of this in the 40 *hadith* (saying, silent approval or action book), which is not the saying of Allah's prophet like the other *hadiths* are, but sayings of Allah, which are not divine decree," the professor continued.

"In this book, Allah tells us that whomever does a thing for his sake and for the sake of someone else together, will have that thing which he has rejected by Allah.

"Further proof of this can be found in the *fatwa* (religious verdict) book, *Fatwa Arkan,* which was written by one of our great sheiks (knowledgeable religious person) and translated by his student ibn Qayyim."

"One more question," Faris said, which caused the doctor to look down at his watch.

The doctor said, "We must hurry, because I have a lecture to give in less than two hours."

"Okay, okay," Faris agreed. "We have been trying to figure out if insurance is a form of *riba* (usury) and, if so, is it okay for us to have insurance, being that we live in American, where that is a must to have on your vehicles."

Doctor Tamimi replied,

"Well, the majority of our scholars are in agreement that insurance is unlawful, however, in India, the Muslim schools and shops are being burned down by Hindus who wish for them to move out of the country all together.

"Being that we are not allowed to take insurance, when our schools, shops and houses are burnt to the ground, the Muslim have no money to rebuild, so they are forced to move on with nothing.

"To make this problem cease, our scholars have declared that, in India, and only in the country of India, that insurance is a thing which the Muslim is allowed to buy.

"This way, when the people who hate us burn down our shops, houses and schools, they will have to pay the money out of their own pockets to rebuild them even bigger and better. This will cause them to cease their barbaric acts."

"Thanks, Sheikh," Faris said, smiling.
He turned and ran off down the same hallway he had traveled down.

The doctor laughed then walked out the front door of the university building and headed towards the parking lot, where his car awaited him. Parked next to his Pontiac were cars that cost over $50,000, making the Pontiac look out of place. It looked as if it belonged in the junkyard, instead of in the parking lot of Howard University, next to the cars of the school's elite.

As he entered his car, he looked at the nearby Maserati with disdain. He could not believe how wasteful people were and how selfishly they went about spending wealth on frivolous things, when most of the children in the world went without clean water or food nearly every day.

He also realized that many of the people in America and elsewhere in the world, were more interested with having heaven on earth, than having heaven in the afterlife. He said to himself,

Do not the people remember that Adam and his wife Hawwa (Eve) were kicked out of heaven and cast down to this earth? If so, then they would understand that this world was not meant to be a place of enjoyment everlasting, but instead a punishment Adam and Eve had to endure for a while to prove that they were worthy of returning back to Paradise.

It was amazing how even those who knew this, still were striving to have heaven in this world, instead of living in this world as travelers, knowing theirs was a temporary journey that could end for anyone at any moment.

Chapter 2

As he stood on the top tier of his prison unit in FCI Edgefield, South Carolina, Tawheed began to feel himself become angry. He felt frustration from dealing with a bunch of grown Muslim who acted as if they didn't notice that the prayer was in; that made him angry.

It had been no more than five minutes earlier that Bari had called the *athani* (call to prayer), which echoed throughout the block. Yet there they stood, watching the women on the BET channel or trying to play out their last hands of Spades.

"Brothers, let's pray."

Bari called the *Iqaman* (second call to prayer) and worked his way in front of the group of eight.

Allahu Akbar Allahu Akbar.

Ash hadu Allah ilah ilallah Wa ahs hadu muhammadar

Rasooluoah

Hayya Alal Salaah Hayya alal Falah qad gama tis Salaah, Qad gama tis Salaah Allahu Akbar Allahu Akbar La iliah ilalah.

When he finished, all the brothers lined up with the backs of their heels joined together and their shoulders touching, in order to leave no gaps in the ranks.

Tawheed then said,

Allah Akbar, and raised his hands to his ears, as the others did the same. It took all of five minutes for them to complete offering the *Sallah* (prayer). Once they did, everyone went back to whatever it was they had been doing before the prayer.

Still frustrated and mad, Tawheed peered over at the other brothers who were still watching TV as if it hadn't been their intention to praise their Lord at all.

He wondered to himself how men who had twenty-four hours in their days were unable to dedicate five minutes of their time to their Lord, whom they called upon for everything.

How ungrateful men were towards their Lord, he thought as he left the old laundry room and headed for the common area. As he passed the brothers, he thought about how they and the prison he was in would soon be behind him.

He turned his back to the world, where he realized his true test would be waiting for him. He was already having doubts about using his daughters' mother's address as his place of residence, especially since he was sure that she still desired him physically.

He also knew, had he not given the parole officer an address, he would have lost his chance of going to the halfway house. That would have meant he would be locked up for six more months, which he was not at all willing to do.

He opened his cell door and went inside, closing the door behind him. Then he began to think about his life and what it would soon be. He believed himself to be patient; anyone who had been placed behind a fence, with a man holding a gun on the other side, might be patient, fearing the latter. But when a man was given a clear road to run wild, would he still choose to be patient?

He believed himself to be capable off suppressing the temptation that would come from dealing with the opposite sex. In a world where the ugliest woman alive looked good, and you risked catching AIDS just to have sex with her, could the horniest man find himself suppressing his desire for sex?

In a matter of hours, he would find out if he was just like many of the other brothers who had studied everything about Islam and grew their beards to their knees, just to help them pass time while they were incarcerated.

Chapter 3

More than six years had passed since the death of his brother, Micheal. Even so, Kent still couldn't shake the pain and anger in his heart for the doctor or his staff who had given his little brother the wrong medication that led to his death.

He looked at Micheal's bed directly across the room from his and began to weep. He wondered, how fair was a God that allowed criminals to run around unchecked, killing innocent people, while an innocent child, who had done nothing wrong to anyone, could lose his life before he even had a chance to live.

He pulled the two automatic pistols from under his mattress then left the room. He walked down the hallway, past his mother, who lay on the couch, sleeping, with a burning cigarette in her hand. He went to her and after removing the cigarette, he pulled the blanket that was mostly on the floor back around her shoulders. He kissed her forehead gently then left the apartment.

"Kent, what's up?"
A group of boys wearing all black boots, jeans and hoodies acknowledged him. He nodded towards them then continued down the hallway towards the stairwell.

Kent was what most well-to-do European Americans considered "white trash." He grew up in the ghetto among blacks, and although he was white, he was very well-respected by all of them.

The respect he received didn't come without struggle. For the first 15 years of his life, he had to fight to prove himself. He was often jumped whenever he got the best of anyone, while the others watching chanted,

"Fight! Fight! A black and a white, if the black don't win, we all jump in!"

Since he stayed in fights, he had become one of the most prized fighters in the entire ghetto. There wasn't a guy there he hadn't fought, at least once. The toughest of the tough guys knew he was a force to be reckoned with.

With his hoodie over his head to conceal his face, he made his way through the sea of thugs who stood covering every inch of the project housing.

Outside of Kent, the only time a white person had the balls to walk through the projects was when they arrived in full force to arrest someone, or when a white junkie came looking for a fix.

After reaching the back of the neighborhood, where a huge fence separated the building from the railroad track, he grabbed the fence and pulled himself up until he reached the top of the gate. Then he dropped over to the other side and began walking down the tracks toward the cemetery where his little brother Micheal's grave was.

The court had found the doctors who were said to be responsible for Michael's death not guilty, leaving Kent and his mother scarred for life.

That let him know that there was no true justice to be found in the court system; he knew that soon enough he would have his vengeance.

Growing up in poverty had allowed him to see some terrible things, like men being murdered in cold blood for nearly nothing. So, at the age of eighteen, there was absolutely nothing at all in his life that he feared, not even God himself, whom Kent had begun to believe did not exist at all.

He reached the cemetery, climbed through a hole in a gate to enter, then traveled across the well-kept grass to his baby brother's tombstone. He pulled what appeared to be a journal out of his pocket and began reading aloud.

After reading three pages, Kent closed the book and began to sob. His little brother Michael had been the only true joy in his life; now that Michael was gone, Kent had become very bitter, dark, and hollow inside.

Kent wiped the tears from his eyes and cheeks then reached into his pocket for a small, stuffed tiger, and put the little toy on top of Michael's headstone. He blew a kiss toward the ground, then turned and walked away.

Chapter 4

Three federal agents hiding among several Muslims in the packed coliseum did their best to record all of what Doctor Tamimi said. Not a word of his speech was lost or distorted by the loud cheers from the audience.

All the agents knew about the doctor was that he was born in the United States to two Palestinian-Americans and he had never been in trouble with the law. None of that mattered at this point, because anyone who was bold enough to speak the name of Allah, after 9/11 was a future terrorist, as far as they were concerned.

"We are in this land, living amongst people who do not believe as we believe but we must still try our best to teach them about the beauty of Islam through our truthful speech and the beauty of our characters.

"We are not a people who will compromise our belief system to please those who do not at all practice that which they themselves claim to believe in.

"If *Esa* (Jesus), the Son of Mary (whom may peace be upon), was here in this land they say is ruled by Christian values, would His followers submit to banishing homosexuality and giving up their belief that He himself is God, the Son of God, or a part of God? Or would they instead kill Him as the people in His time aimed to do?"

The crowd erupted into cheers as the agents sat, uncomfortable and dressed in traditional Muslim *throbs* (long T-shirts). Agent Fawks, the smallest of the three men, pulled at the long beard he had grown in order to blend in with Muslim men and not be detected as the hypocrite he was. He said to the other two agents,

"There's no way that you're gonna tell me that this guy is not a Jihadi."

"I think we're wasting our time and the country's money watching all these god-fearing people," Agent Felts said.

He was a huge, reddish-colored man who stretched his arms as he spoke. Agent Wise, the superior officer in the group, turned his attention back to the doctor, who hadn't stopped speaking. As he turned around, Agent Wise said,

"No matter what it is that you two think, or don't think, the bosses say that we watch him, so we watch him."

Chapter 5

For over three years, the three agents had been watching Doctor Tamimi and many of the other men within the Islamic community in Washington, DC. They were beginning to hate watching. So, they did not blow their cover, every day, five times a day, they each entered the *masjic* to pray. They even ate at Middle Eastern restaurants, which allowed them to keep an eye on many of the men they were watching, without making those men becoming suspicious or aware they were being investigated.

Agent Wise figured that whoever was stupid enough to pretend to be Muslim had mental issues that professional help couldn't fix for them. He was already tired of pretending to be Muslim; all his co-workers felt the same.

Each day, after the three of them had prayed two *Rakats* (units of prayer); they turned their heads to face right and ended their prayers with *tasleem* (saying *As Salaamu Alaikum Wa Rahmatullah)*. Then the three of them rose and crossed the floor of the *Musalla* (prayer area) and entered past the *Wudu* (purification station), before going outside. There was a large gathering of worshippers who milled around and purchased things from the merchants who set up outside the mosque.

Doing their best to blend into the crowd, the agents smiled and said, *Salaamu Alaikum*, to each person they passed. They even pretended to make *Thikra* (supplication in the form of *Subhana Allah* (glory to

23

Allah); *Alham du lillah* (All praise be to Allah); and *Allahu Akbar* (Allah is greatest), which was the ritual all Muslims completed after praying.

The agents secretly recorded everyone's comings and goings, in and out of the *masjid*, but since the *Muslimas* (Muslim sisters) entered through another door at the back of the *masjid*, and prayed on the top level of the mosque, above the men and behind a barrier, it was difficult for the agents to know who was on that level. It was also difficult for them to know who had made it into the *masjid* from the back door, where men were restricted from entering at all.

"They sure as hell got us beat on this sexist thing," Agent Wise said, as he watched the fully-garbed women entering the *masjid* through the back entrance.

"It's not a sexist thing at all," Agent Feltz said. "And if you had studied what it is that these people actually believe in, you would know that."
He thought about how to get a female agent into the *masjid* to spy on the Muslim women since the male agents were denied access of any kind.

"Just as we are, men of every walk of life are weak for the opposite sex and when you place a bunch of men and women in a room together, eyes are gonna start wandering," Feltz said.

"These people try their best to focus on Allah alone; to do so, they separate themselves from the opposite sex. If a woman were to bend over in front of any of us right now, we'd be looking, so if a woman bends over in front of a man who is praying, then his intention will no longer be on god, but on what's in front of him. This is the reason why the women are ordered to walk behind men, as well."

Feltz continued, "It's nearly impossible for us to lower our gaze from that thing, and you know exactly what I'm talking about when I say, 'that thing.'"

"My god, Brad," Agent wise said, looking at Feltz with anger in his eyes. "You're starting to sound as if you're becoming one of them."

"In order to understand what it is you are looking at, you must understand everything about it, like what it eats, how it thinks, why it prays, and more," Feltz replied. He continued,

"I know that to Muslims everything about a woman is a distraction to the opposite sex, just as it is to us. A woman's voice causes a man to look away from whatever he's doing to see what it is she looks like. The sound of her footsteps causes men to chase a woman like a ghost.

"It seems that everything about women calls you to give

attention to them, and if it is calling you to her attention and you're her husband, then what does that say about the other poor bastards who are unable to have her, but want her, as well?"

Wise said, "Hell, I have trouble focusing whenever your wife Angela comes into the room where we play poker. Those short shorts, that cut right into her, and her long, flowing hair and perfume fills the whole room." He told Feltz,

"I always thought you had her do that intentionally, to cause everyone to lose focus so you could beat us out of all them card games."

Laughing, Feltz said, "I had no idea that you were secretly making love to Angie with your eyes while I was taking all your money."

Agent Roberts said, "I guess I know now why Sherly left me."

He lowered his head towards the ground as a group of men walked by. All the agents stopped talking. When the men were past them, Wise asked,

"Hell, boy, if you thought Angie looked good in them jeans when you met her, how do you think the rest of us felt about her?"

"It always confused me how a woman could dress so sexy to cause you to look at her, but she didn't expect you to look at another woman with bigger breasts and a wider set of hips once she had you," Wise said.

"And that's probably going to be the reason why me and my wife won't last," Feltz laughed.

"Ya'll will make it; I'm sure of it," said Wise.

"I don't know. I fell in love with the way she looked and ten years later, she's not looking the same. A lot of times, I see women who are sexier than she is, so it's only a matter of time, I figure."

Wise looked around to make sure that his comments couldn't be heard by anyone outside of the circle of three, then he said,

"Speaking of beauties, I sure would like to see how fine one of these *Jahadi* women are, up under all of those sheets."

As the three agents stood talking to one another, a beautiful voice echoed through the loudspeaker on top of the mosque.

Allah Akbar (Allah is greatest) *Allahu Akbar* (Allah is greatest). *Allahu Akbar Allahu Akbar.*

Ash hadu ils ilaha ilallah (I bear witness there is no god but Allah) *Ash hadu alla ilaha illallah.*

Ash hadu anna Muhammadar Rasoolulah (I bear witness that Muammad is the messenger and last slave prophet of god) *Ash hadu anna Muhammadar Rasoolulah*

Hayya alas Salaah (Come to prayer)

Hayya alas Salaah, Hayya alal Falah (Come to success) *Hayya alal Falah*

Allahu Akbar Allahu Akbar La ilaha ila Allah

The calling was called the *Athan* (call to prayer) and the one who had called it was the *Mu azzin*. When he had finished, everyone who was still standing outside the mosque went inside for the *Jumauh* (Friday prayer), including the three agents.

As the *Imam* (religious leader) or *Khateeb* (speaker), as he was also known, made his way upon the *Minbar* (pulpit), everyone looked in his direction and waited for him to give the *Kutbah* (religious speech). He began,

"Today is the day that Allah created Adaam. Today is the day that Adaam died; it is the day that he and his wife were kicked out of Paradise and this day will also be the day that the world will end and all of us will be resurrected.

"Many people on earth are of the assumption that when we die we are going to go in the ground and go to sleep to rest in peace, as if we never did a thing wrong or right that we must still have to be held accountable for.

28

"Do we really think that all of these prophets and messengers have frivolously come here, telling us what it is that our Lord has said we can and cannot do, just for us to disobey them in all of this, and not be punished or rewarded for listening to them in it?

"We will not just die and rest in peace. No! Every last one of us will be held accountable for our actions, whether small or huge. We have a bill to pay and it shall be paid by us either in this life or the next."

As he continued to talk, the three agents couldn't help but hear what it was he said, even if their sole intention was to be there for another reason entirely.

Chapter 6

Kent sprawled across the roof of the building directly across for the hospital where his brother Micheal died. He stared thorough the scope of a Remington 700 sniper rifle.

His eyes burned from forcing himself not to blink, but he refused to abandon his position or mission until his target crossed his sight.

Being so focused on the office window of Doctor Sanford, Kent hadn't even noticed the man get out of his car and enter the front of the hospital. As the doctor walked through the lobby and towards the elevator, he smiled and looked at the gorgeous shape of one of the younger nurses, as she bent over to help a child who was a patient.

Feeling as if he had not a worry in the world, Doctor Sandford entered the elevator and rode to the eleventh floor, where his office was located. He exited the elevator and strolled down the hallway; he whistled a tune to himself that nobody else could hear.

Once he reached his office, he swiped his key card and waited for the door to unlock. He entered his office but didn't turn on the light, even though he had done so every day from the last twelve and a half years he had worked at the hospital.

Kent could feel his palms sweating. He thought about giving up but knew that if he did, he would more than likely never return.

Just then, he saw a figure take a seat behind the desk of Dr. Sandford. Without thinking about it twice, Kent squeezed the trigger, fired two rounds, then watched as the figure slumped over in the seat. He quickly gathered his weapon, climbed off the roof and left the rooftop, making sure no one had seen him exit.

Chapter 7

"So how did you like the *khutbah*," Faris asked his younger brother Talat.

After leaving the *Masjid Dar Al-Hijrahsi* parking lot, Faris turned left on the highway. His younger brother was not so impressed. He turned his head to the right as they came to a red light and said,

"All they do is talk about how to get to heaven. They never tell you how to have the good in this life, as well."

Talat had turned his head just in time to see a female.

"Wow, look at how good she looks. Isn't it *Alhamdu lillah* for such a beautiful creature?"

Faris turned his head in the direction that had diverted his brother's attention and he saw a very pretty Muslim woman with green eyes. She was driving a green Porsche.

"She has to be the one for me," Talat said.

He rolled down his window and began waving to get her attention.

"What are you doing..." was all he asked before Faris powered the window back up and pulled over into another lane.

"First of all, that could be someone's wife."

"Yeah, she might be my wife if you stop hating on me and

pull the car back over where she's at," Talat said, frustrated by what his brother had done.

"All women have rights, even the Christian women; even though they don't hold the men of this society to giving them their rights, they have rights. So, you know that our women have rights that *Allah* has ordered for us to give them," Faris explained, adding,

"That's not some hood rat you're talking to, so don't dare approach her as if she was one. Besides, you wouldn't have wanted that sister anyway."

"You don't know what I would have wanted, and if I did have a chance with her, now it's gone," Talat said.

He was frustrated and folded his arms across his chest.

"The girl was wearing a head scarf and an *Abaya* (full body covering), while she was listening to Fifty Cent rappin,' telling her to take her clothes off," Faris explained. "If she wasn't confused, then she should be made aware that she is a walking contradiction."

"Man, everybody's not perfect like your wife Khadijah, and since you're already married, you have no idea of the way I struggle every day."

"If I do as the Quran says, and lower my gaze by looking away from one woman, here comes another one, looking just as sexy and even more provocative. I would have to walk around with my hand over my eyes just to prevent myself from looking at all these women," Talat said.

He turned his attention to a group of women walking up the hill towards Northern Virginia Community College, where he himself attended school.

"If you're having such a hard time controlling your desire for the opposite sex, then just start fasting."

"I've been fasting so much that I'm lighter than a feather. Besides, it doesn't work at times, either."

"Well, you need to go to Dad and ask him to allow you to get married."

"Are you crazy? Every time I have mentioned something to him about getting married, he tells me to finish school first. It'll be ten years before I complete school, and then I'll have to buy a house and have so much money in the bank to take care of a family."

Talat continued, "It would just be better if I done like the

Christians and just got some random girl who I'd probably never see again and just do it."

Faris wouldn't have that. He pointed his finger into his little brother's face,

"Shut up! You shut up talking like that right now! We are Muslim! We are not like these people who run around doing everything and anything they choose to do just because it feels like the right thing to do.

"What will the woman who lets you use her up tell the man she marries? Do you think he still will even want her after learning that she's given herself to you and other men in every way that he deserves to touch and see her?"

Talat came back, "This is America. People are sharing wives with each other like it's nothing, so I really don't see what's the problem, anyways."

"The problem is that you will be disobeying your Lord. What if this woman gets pregnant? Or gives you some disease? Do you think that will be worth the small amount of time it took you to take down her pants?"

"I'm not gonna catch a disease or have a baby by any of these girls. I just wanna do it to them, like everyone else is."

"Ok, so after you do it to her, like everyone else has, are you gonna take her to Dad and see if he will allow you to marry her?"

"Why are you being so difficult? I told you that I just wanna have my way with her, then get rid of her. These women are not to be made into wives; they are just good for a good time."

"So, you mean to tell me that they are good enough to pleasure you but not be your wife or someone worthy of being introduced to your family?"

"I'm not gonna just marry some girl that has probably had sex with the whole college, or several of my friends, so they can all be laughin' at me behind my back."

Faris pulled up to the front of the school and Talat opened his door and got out. Faris asked him,

"If a man comes up to you and says *Alhamdu lillah* for a beautiful creation, and he is staring at your wife the way you were staring at that sister, would it be okay with you?"

Talat, who was offended by the question, slammed the door and headed towards the front of the school. When he entered the building, away from his brother's eyes, he started looking at all the thighs of every woman wearing tight jeans and passing him. He had imagined many of them intimately a few times when he had

41

masturbated; he would have them in real life if he did not get married soon.

How could anyone focus on school with so many gorgeous, provocatively dressed women all around him, he wondered. He walked up the stairs and headed toward his class.

How could he be wrong for wanting the women when it was them who were enticing him sexually, and every other man to want them, too. He thought about Sudan, his birthplace, wishing he was there, instead of in a classroom.

He knew he would never be able to make it another year without becoming one of the fornicators if he stayed in America.

A friend of his was coming out of the restroom, and asked,

"What's up Talat?"

The eyes of both boys were glued to the back sides of two girls who stood a few feet in front of them. Talat had known Tyrone for two years. His friend smiled at the woman who was staring back at him, then said,

"What I wouldn't do for a piece of that."

Talat thought, *if he can do it, then I can do it* as he walked into his classroom.

Chapter 8

Safa, who was from Morocco, was not only very smart, she also was stunningly beautiful. As she was Muslim, she was very seldom allowed to do many of the things her friends from school did, like hanging out late, wearing what she wanted, and going to parties.

Safa believed, rightly, that her parents had never participated in parties, or drinking. She concluded they could not tell her whether the effects of such things were always bad, although they often did tell her so.

Her friends drank, smoked and wore tight clothes. None of them had dropped out of school or had car accidents that resulted in injuries to themselves or others.

In Morocco, it was normal for women to not go to clubs and not dress in tight, revealing clothing. In America, those were the norm and Safa was tired of feeling as if she was an outsider inside her new country.

She had promised her friends she would meet them at Club Shadows and there she sat, parked less than a block away. She still couldn't bring herself to get out of the car. *Everything will be alright,* she told herself, trying to pump herself up to get out of the car. Again, she looked in the mirror and wondered if she was really as beautiful as she had been told many times by her friends and others.

She removed her head scarf and her *Abaya*, revealing the sexy pair of thighs she had been hiding from public view all her life. She got out of the car, locked her doors, and boldly strutted down the sidewalk towards the club. As she passed a huge office building, she caught a glimpse of herself in the reflective windows. She stopped in her tracks. She was taken aback by what she saw; a beautiful, very well-shaped young woman.

"Wow," said a group of men who were across the street and looking at her.

She smiled, then began walking and stopped when she was in front of the club where a hundred other women, dressed even sexier than she was, stood in line, waiting to be admitted. She was confused about what to do next, so she stood on the corner and tried to blend in. Kent, who was crossing the street, spotted her and came towards her. He said,

"What's up, beautiful?"

He put his arm around her waist, but she pulled herself away from him.

"So, you can stand there, looking all sexy, and making me want you, but you're not willing to share what it is you're tempting me with, right?"

Kent licked his lips and smiled while he looked her up and down.

"Do you know Shaheedah or Ramona," Safa asked.

She turned to hide her booty from view, as Kent and the other men standing near the club stared at her, never even blinking. Kent winked at her and said,

"Yeah, I know them. They're both in the club, waiting on me."

"Can you take me in there to see them?"

Safa lowered her gaze from Kent's face. He said,

"Sure. Come on."

He grabbed her hand and they worked their way to the front of the line. He whispered something in the bouncer's ear, then handed the man $50. The bouncer moved the rope to the side and allowed them to enter. They climbed stairs that led into the club. Once inside, Kent leaned into Safa and said,

"I have to hold you tight, because as you can see, it's a crowd of people and its dark in there. So, if you don't let me hold you close, you're gonna get lost and me or your friends won't be able to find you in this sea of people."

Reluctantly, she allowed him to place his arm around her waist. When he did, she began to regret ever coming to the club. As she was regretting each moment of her decision, she figured that once she was with her friends, she would feel better about coming there.

She was glad the club was dark. She feared someone from the Moroccan community or her school would see her inside the club. As she and Kent worked their way through the crowd and up the stairs to the VIP section, she thought, if someone went back and told her dad she was up in the club, dressed so sexy, he would never forgive her. Once they reached the VIP area, Kent sat down across from her and asked,

"Is this better?"

"Where are my friends? I thought you said they were already in here, waiting on you."

"Yeah, I guess they went to the restroom or something."
Kent pulled a tiny bag of powder cocaine from his pocket and began to sniff. He looked at Safa's breasts and asked,

"Would you like some?"

"No, I'm good. I don't do drugs," she said, trying to pull her shirt over her cleavage to keep him from staring.

"Here. At least have a drink. It tastes just like fruit juice and it has very low alcohol content. You'll only feel a slight buzz."

Safa took the cupful of Alize he had poured for her and slowly began to sip from it. When she saw that it really did taste like fruit juice, she drank more and more until her cup was empty.

"Is that your friends right there?"

Kent diverted her attention so he could pour a "roofie" (Rohypnol, a common date rape drug) in her cup, along with more of the Alize.

"Where are they? I don't seem them," she said after turning back to face him.

"Look, finish your cup then we'll go over to the girls' room, where I'm sure they must have gone."

Kent looked away from her, so she would feel more comfortable. She began to drink from her newly-filled glass; as soon as she emptied it, he stood up and said,

"Come on, let's go find your friends."

As she stood, she felt herself floating. It was a pleasant sensation that made her think she didn't have a worry in the world. She walked to the stairs they had climbed to get into the VIP section, and stumbled down them, with Kent pulling her along by the hand. They passed a crowd of people and came to an empty, secluded area.

He looked in her eyes; and that's when he knew he had her. She had an off look in her eyes and it told him she was no longer in control of herself. He grabbed her and slammed her against the wall. She started to panic. He began undoing her jeans as she begged him to stop. She tried to fight him off, but for some reason she had no strength. Instead, she felt like she was outside her body.

Seeing her luscious, bare thighs and the diamond between them caused Kent's blood to flow. As she cried, he had his way with her, over and over again, until she begged *Allah* to make him stop. Once he finished pleasuring himself with her, he climbed off and left her on the ground. She balled herself into the fetal position and cried.

He knew no one would ever believe he had raped her, since the whole club had seen the two of them together from the moment they walked in. He laughed while he walked outside; he felt untouchable.

Safa, on the other hand, knew she would not be able to report what happened to her family or the police; for fear that her father would discover she had disobeyed him by going to the club in the first place. She also knew if anyone learned what had happened to her, she would be regarded, from that moment on, as a lewd, fornicating woman who was quick to participate in *haram* (forbidden acts).

Chapter 9

It had only been three weeks since Tawheed came home from federal prison. Already he was starting to realize it had been much easier to be a good Muslim in jail, than it was in the world. On the outside, there were no brothers to lift you up about praying or lusting. No one knew if you were attending *jumauh* or not; no one was able to see if you were slacking, or not.

All one had to do in the streets was cut of their beard and they could just as easily blend in with the disbelievers. That made it impossible for anyone to see the wrong they were doing on a daily basis. Still, no matter how hard it was to do right on the outside, Tawheed wasn't willing to go back to prison for even an hour.

He sat on the couch, wrapping his daughter ShuQurans's head in a traditional Muslim woman's head scarf. He watched her mother, Dawn, who always seemed to wear nothing more than her bra and panties around the house when he was there. She entered the living room, stopped and stood over top of them.

"I told you I don't like my daughter dressing like that. She ain't no Muslim," she said.
As she spoke, she spread her thighs in front of him, making him bite his lip. He wanted her badly, but he refused to allow her to turn him back into a fornicator after he had gone so many years doing what was right.

He had offered to marry her while he was in prison, but when she refused to learn about Islam, he decided it would be best if they weren't married.

As she ran her hand down her thigh, trying to entice him, he began to regret ever using her address as his own home address. He couldn't stop her from walking around her house dressed as she saw fit, but he could stop himself from sleeping with her. He knew if he slept with her that his chance of finding a good Muslim wife would be over before it started.

What brother would allow him, a fornicator, to marry their daughter, he wondered. He stood up and looked at himself in the mirror to his right. Then he looked at his daughter, who looked absolutely amazing, covered as she should have always been.

"Where you taking my daughter?"

"We're going to the mosque, Mommy," ShuQuran said, smiling as she hugged Tawheed.

"I'm coming too, then."

"Cool, you can come but you're gonna have to cover up like she is," Tawheed said, looking in her eyes.

"I ain't gonna cover nothing. This ain't no Saudi Arabia, its America, so I'm going in there with the tightest, sexiest shortest skirt that I can find," she said.

She strutted through the kitchen, then down the hallway to her bedroom. He knew that he and she would be thrown out of the *masjid* on their heads if she showed up dressed like she said she would. He picked up ShuQuran and lifted her to his chest, then walked to the front door.

"What about Mommy?"

Dawn was slipping into a skirt that barely covered her thighs. She heard her daughter's voice and looked out of the bedroom at them. As Tawheed opened the front door to leave, Dawn called out,

"If you leave me, Ima tell your parole officer that you don't really live here and get your butt locked up before the day is out!"

He looked down at ShuQuran, shook his head, and went back to the couch. He waited for Dawn, knowing he would be late for the prayer.

As he watched her get dressed, he felt himself being turned on by her. He shook the thought from his head. Being from the streets meant he still had a lot of evil in his heart that he hadn't suppressed. Being with her only meant he would not have anyone to save him from himself, if and when he became weak.

Everything he stood for now, she stood against. It would be impossible to try raising children up under a house that had two

55

contradicting sets of rules that governed it. He thought about how Dawn was acting towards him and he knew, when he told her he was going to marry a Muslim woman, she would really try to get him thrown back in jail. He thought it would be better to wait until he got his own place.

As he sat there, impatiently waiting on Dawn to finish getting dressed, he answered as many questions as he could that ShuQuran was asking him about Islam. At that moment, he was extremely happy he had spent his time studying his *deen* (way of life), instead of playing cards or watching TV while he was locked up.

Chapter 10

He sat behind the dumpster in an alley directly across from her building, watching her do what she had done every single day, from the moment he began observing her.

She left the building and went down the steps to the curb that ran the length of the street where she lived. Without a care in the world, she bent over, stretching her legs, arms and back, preparing for her early morning jog.

He looked toward her in rage, thinking about Micheal, who had been alive and happy before she and the many others who agreed to help him selfishly snatched his beautiful, innocent life from him, instead.

He would soon inflict his vengeance on her, the same as he had done with the others. But she would not die quickly. No, he wanted to enjoy every moment of making her suffer. Maybe he would get her pregnant, so she could give him a son to replace the baby brother she had taken from him so many years ago.

As he watched her, he could feel himself wanting her. She was beautiful; from her appearance, one would have figured her to be innocent, but he knew better. She was a killer who had taken the life of the only brother he had, and for that, she would soon pay dearly.

He watched as she began to job. As she did, he took off running and watched her travel the same route she took every single day, a route he had memorized like the back of his own hand.

Chapter 11

Life hadn't turned out at all the way he had planned it; it was starting to get the best of him. He was tired of hearing Dawn yelling threats about getting him locked up again if he didn't do this or do that. It seemed they argued every day about him teaching their daughter about Islam. He had known he should have kept the secret from her, that he wanted to marry a Muslim woman. But when she continued trying to force herself upon him every night, he let her know why he was refusing to share her bed with her.

Six months had passed since the day he was released from prison and he was no closer to getting married like he had so wished and intended to do. His job was even beginning to bother him. Not only was he not getting paid what he knew the job was worth, but also many women who worked in the same office he did were very vocal about what it was they wanted to do with him.

After spending eight years doing nothing but working out, Tawheed could understand how they would want him in such a manner, but he didn't understand why his boss, who was also a woman, could hold the fact that she wanted him over his head.

Work was no longer about work; it had become the question of whether he was willing to give in to the desires of a bunch of sexy, horny women he was undoubtedly attracted to, so he could keep his job. He figured that after a week or so the women's desires for him would fade, but his paying no attention to them just seemed to make them more emboldened in their pursuit of him. The pressure of it all was beginning to get the best of him. He got up from the couch and walked into the kitchen; he figured he would have a late-night snack.

When he opened the refrigerator door, he noticed a bottle of Hennessey on one of the shelves. Consuming alcohol was forbidden in Islam, so he knew better, and to think twice about drinking. He knew that the person who became intoxicated wouldn't have his prayers answered by their Lord for forty days. That's something he couldn't afford.

He thought to himself, *I'm already living with a woman I am not married to, which is already forbidden in Islam. Every day, I lust for nearly every woman I see, so how bad will it be to take a drink.* He figured one drink would surely not put him in the hellfire. He reached in and took the bottle of brown liquid from the refrigerator. With the bottle dangling from his hand, he returned to the couch.

After getting comfortable again on the couch, he unscrewed the top and brought the bottle up to his lips. At first, he sipped the liquor; then he guzzled it until his chest began to burn. He laughed, feeling instant relief.

Everything will be alright, he figured, as he took another drink, then another. Before long, the bottle was half-empty and he was feeling drunker than he had ever felt in his life. He closed his eyes and began to dream of the Muslim wife he would soon have.

She was so real he could feel her touching him, as if they were together in real life. He couldn't believe what she was doing as he felt himself inside of her, knowing his wet dream was a gift to him for not masturbating for so many years. Just as he was about to climax, he could hear her calling his name and feel her kiss his bare chest. The dream felt so real; he thought it had to be more of a vision than a dream, as he felt himself exploding. He held her and smiled, feeling as if he had finally received the reward that came with being patient.

The next morning, Tawheed woke to a terrible headache. He couldn't believe he drank the Hennessey. When he forced his eyes open to see the clock next to him, he realized he had missed not just the *Fajr* (early dawn prayer), but he also had missed the *Zuhr* (afternoon prayer), as well.

He rubbed his eyes, attempting to get his blurred vision in order. That's when he saw what he had feared most. The dream he had was not a dream at all. Next to him was Dawn, naked and asleep with her legs wrapped around his waist. There was no doubt about it. Now he was ruined.

He jumped up from the couch and raced to the bathroom, stumbling across the floor and nearly tripping over his own feet. Once inside, he closed the bathroom door, then turned to look at himself in the mirror.

He wondered, *What have I done?* He began to feel as if he had just destroyed everything he had been praying and hoping for. He thought to himself, *How will I be able to get married to a Muslim woman now? What if Dawn, who he was sure had been with other men the entire time he was in prison, had given him a disease? What if Dawn became pregnant from last night?*

The more he thought, the more he began to wish that he was back in prison, where he was safe from the evil he had just committed. He turned on the water in the tub, then stepped in it. He began performing a *Ghusl* (full body) shower while asking Allah to forgive him. It was only one time, he figured, but he still couldn't convince himself that what he had done would go without regret.

His own father had made babies by more than seven women and had gone to prison for twenty years. None of the kids' mothers liked each other, so Tawheed never got to know his brothers and sisters at all. The results of that had been fatal, in more ways than one.

His older brother, Khalfeed, had been murdered when he was only fourteen. As everyone sat in the church for his funeral, his father, who had only seen Khalfeed one time, was escorted inside by two deputy marshals. Everyone watched in tears.

After kissing his dead son's forehead, his father turned to face his daughter, who was sitting with her fiancé, also his son. He went to her and said,

"I'm glad to see that you and your brother are there for each other."

His daughter and son, who until that moment had no idea they were brother and sister, just sat there in shock, just like everyone else in the church. But even that hadn't been the worst of what was to come. He would later come to find out that it had been one of his youngers sons who had killed his own older brother, the oldest son. More than likely, had they known they were brothers, the murder would not have happened at all.

Tawheed's head was pounding, the more he thought about what might come about from his decision to get drunk. *All it took was one mistake to ruin your entire life*, he thought. He listened as Dawn entered the bathroom and went to the tub.

Chapter 12

The month of *Ramadan* (burning) was a fasting that extended twenty-nine to thirty days. Tawheed was extremely grateful when it began. His fasting was a valid excuse to not touch Dawn at all. She had knowledge of what a Muslim was or wasn't supposed to be doing during *Ramadan,* or any other important time, so Tawheed scolded her severely when she tried to complain that he would not share the bed with her. Going to bed with her was something Tawheed could not stop doing since they slept together the night he got drunk. He figured the situation he got himself into with her was only temporary, and that turned out to be true, after all.

He was spending most of his time in the *masjid* around people who had grown up in Muslim countries. The way they thought and acted convinced Tawheed that he hadn't been on the level he thought he was on during all the time he was in prison. The brother Talat, whom he had met while attending the *masjid*, had encouraged him to seek further education; now, like Talat, he was taking college classes, as well.

The Muslims had also helped him find a new job and a place to stay, but he had yet to get permission from his parole officer to move there. He had to tread lightly with Dawn; he knew that as soon as she caught wind of his decision to move, she would threaten to take his daughter completely out of his life or kick him out of her house. He'd lose his "place of residence" if that happened.

Ramadan on the street was a million times better than it had been in prison. Every night he broke his fast, one of the brothers would invite him to their homes to eat with them and their families. They all treated him as if he was some rare jewel that they were very proud to have around as much as they were able. He was really surprised by how much love the brothers from overseas showed him. One evening he whispered to his friend,

"Talat, it's almost time to pray."

Talat sat at the desk next to his and was reading his American History book. He looked at his watch and, after closing the book, rose from his seat and headed out of the classroom with Tawheed following him. They both entered a restroom where they performed *wudu* (purification), then found a secluded corner of the building that faced east.

Tawheed lined up where the person who was to lead the prayer was supposed to be, but Talat said,

"You should get over here so that you'll be on my right."

Giving Talat a funny look, Tawheed asked,

"Why would I do that, when I'm leading you in prayer?"

"Well, actually, I'm quite sure that it's closer to the *sunna* that I lead you in prayer, instead."

With slight arrogance in his tone and looking down at Talat, Tawheed replied,

"You're only like eighteen, right?"

"I'm seventeen, but age only matters after three things, which are: if you and I know the same amount of Quran; if you and I recite it the same; and if you and I have performed *Hajj* at the same time."

Tawheed figured there was no way that Talat, who was only seventeen, knew more Quran than he did, so to show him that he wasn't smarter than he was, he looked at him and said,

"I've memorized over thirty *surahs* of the Quran."

"Well then, you need to line up on my right," Talat said, moving into the position Tawheed was in.

With a confused look on his face, Tawheed said,

"How much of the Quran do you know?"

"In my country, most children memorize the Quran by age eight. We memorize the Quran before the ink it is written with even dries. So, to answer your question, I have memorized all of it."

Tawheed, who had been one of the brothers in prison who had spent his time studying, had memorized more Quran than most of the brothers there, which led to his slight arrogance. Now, he had been humbled to his core by a seventeen-year-old boy who was not just more knowledgeable than he was, but whose character was better than that of anyone he had met in his life.

He placed his heel next to Talat's and stood shoulder to shoulder with him. They began praying. After the *salaat*, Tawheed looked into Talat's eyes and asked,

"Why do you brothers treat me so kind? I mean, you don't even know me and I'm not from where either of you are from."

Talat's face began to glow as a smile came across it. Once he had finished thinking, he looked at Tawheed and said,

"Unlike the rest of us, whose family and cultures expect us to be Muslim; you have chosen to be Muslim on your own, with no one to encourage you to do so, at all.

"You are an American man who can do everything his heart desires, but still, you have chosen to submit to the will of your Lord. That goes against everything you have been taught.

"This could only be because you sincerely believe and this is something which is rare, even in many Muslim countries. You have so many sisters who cover themselves, only because it is what is expected of them, culturally. Brothers who have come to this country don't even grow their beards as they should, because they want to make people think they are not Muslim.

"When the man who has known the truth his entire life chooses to hide his Islam, while a man who knows that people in his country have a slight dislike for Muslims, based on what they hear about us in the media, and based on what they have heard about 9/11, chooses to let his Islam be illuminated without shame, how can one man not love to see this?

"Be grateful to Allah for choosing to guide you to the truth, Tawheed. Pay attention to the signs that he is showing you. You are the only Muslim in your family, so you have been blessed to be guided out of everyone. How can you not feel blessed every day?"

"Yeah, I know I'm blessed but as you have said, I am alone in my striving, which makes my journey very difficult.

"I pray that Allah gives me a Muslim wife and I mean a real Muslim wife, not just a sister who covers herself in order to please her family or be culturally correct."

"Trust me," Talat said, standing up. "I know exactly what you mean. Let me show you something."

Talat led Tawheed to the front door of the classroom where they were supposed to be.

"Look at that sister. She is so beautiful, and I believe that maybe she is even a descendent of our beloved prophet," he said, signaling with his head towards a very young sister sitting next to the door.

"Why don't you tell her how you feel and state your intentions to marry her?"

"It's not that easy," Talat said.

75

With a melancholy face, he turned away from the window in the classroom door. Just then, the students began standing up, gathering their things, and leaving the classroom. Tawheed watched as the *Muslimah* left, too. He could tell she was well-educated and very shy.

"Excuse me, sister, *Salaamu Alaikum*," he said.

She turned to face him and he walked toward her. He looked at Talat, who couldn't believe what he was doing. Talat turned away; his heart began pounding away in his chest.

"Yes, my brother, how may I help you," she asked Tawheed, lowering her gaze to the floor.

"Look, I need to know if you are married and if you're not, you need to know that Talat, my friend who is right over there, is in love with you to the point where he can't even stay focused on his studies.

"He wants to ask you to marry him but he is shy, so here I am asking you on his behalf."

She blushed but tried her best not to give away that fact that she had waited a long time for Talat to state his intentions to marry her. She had known him for two years, but never once had he even looked at her. She wrote a number on a piece of paper, then said,

"Here is my father's number. Have him call him today, around 5pm."

"Thank you," Tawheed said.

Smiling, he returned to Talat.

Chapter 13

Saadiq smiled when he saw Tawheed's name at the top of the letter the correctional officer handed him. He anxiously returned to his cell, then opened the letter. He began to read what his friend had to say to him. As he read, his smile turned into a frown. He was heartbroken to hear about the tests his friend was enduring and failing.

Saadiq had a life sentence. He would never be free. At that moment, reading Tawheed's letter, he was glad, knowing that by way of the prison, his Lord had favored him.

He knew, if he made it back to the world, he would kill many more men and have his way with as many women who would spread their legs for him.

In prison, he was strong, but he also realized that it was due to him being around other brothers who were a constant reminder of what it was he was doing. Shaheed, a brother who also had a life sentence, peeked into the cell.

"You ready?"

"*Na am* (yes)," Saadiq replied in Arabic. He got up from his bed and went outside the cell.

The two men walked outside and across the rec yard, then they entered the law library where the other members of the *Majlis* (gathering) were waiting.

Sunni, who was the prison *Imam* (prayer leader), opened with a supplication in Arabic. It translated to wishing peace upon the prophet and his companions. Then he asked,

"So, what exactly are the issues in the community that need to be addressed here today?"

Luqman, who was the *Shareef* (head of security), looked around at all the faces in the circle, then he said,

"One of the officers continues to remove the brothers' Qurans from the place in which they put them. Because of that, many of the brothers have become angry to the point where they are thinking about resorting to violence.

"I have talked to the brothers and a lot of them have the attitude that, since the officers are privileged to go home every day, and they themselves have to be in here for the rest of their lives, they feel they should just simply show these officers how much they have to lose.

"Brothers have the opinion that if they kill these officers, nothing will happen, because they will not even be around to finish the first sentence, then have to worry about another one they may get for doing it."

Sunni lightly stroked the bottom of his beard with his right hand. He looked up into the faces of all the men who sat next to him and said,

"Tell the brothers to be patient with what they are going through with this officer and let them know that I will talk to the captain about this individual on mainline tomorrow. Are there any more issues?"

"Yes, we have found out that one of the brothers is gambling again and we just paid his debt for more than $1500."

"Pay his debt again, then walk him up to the Special Housing Unit. Make sure that is done as soon as you go back."

"Imam, if we are checking him in, I don't see the reason for us having to pay his debt, as well."

"Those who do not pay their debts will be held up from entering into Paradise; also the people he owes may intend to take us to war behind this money, which means a lot of men will be stabbed over a small amount of money that we can afford to pay.

"We never want anyone to say that the Muslims do not pay their debts. Now, if there are no more issues, this meeting is adjourned."

The Imam recited in Arabic to close out the group setting.

As the brothers went back to their blocks, they saw every prison officer head towards B House. Through the glass windows in the gym, they could see three offices lying on the ground. The brothers watched in horror as Saleem, an elderly brother who also had a life sentence, was escorted to the SHU (Special Housing Unit). There was blood all over his hands and clothes.

Luqman could see that Saleem had two knives taped to his hands. They would later find out that he had gotten tired of the officer moving his Quran and had decided to kill him, along with the officer standing next to him.

Chapter 14

As she stood there, nearly out of breath, she sipped from the water bottle in her hand. Becky had no idea that what she feared the most wasn't far from her. Like the cheetah in the wild, hunting for a gazelle or some other animal near where he is prowling, Kent sprang out of the woods along the bike trail. He had a butcher knife in his hand and Becky jumped when she saw him with it.

He grabbed her before she could take off running. For fear of losing her life, she kneed him in the groin and he fell to the ground. He grabbed her long pony tail and held her in a death grip. She fell to the ground on top of him. She screamed as the knife blade pierced her side, going deep into her ribcage.

The sound of her screams could be heard for a distance and echoed through the woods surrounding the bike trail. Dr. Tamimi, who was in his house not far from where the attack was happening, went to his wife. He heard the screams of a woman coming from his back yard.

"Call the police," he said, turning to his wife.

He left the room and quickly walked downstairs. Once he reached the first floor, he went into the kitchen and pulled a knife from a drawer. He went out of the back door and ran towards where the screams were coming from.

He carefully moved towards the woods behind his house and to the bike trail the woods concealed. He no longer heard screaming, but he continued forward, feeling in his gut that something was wrong. As he broke the tree line, he saw her, lying naked on the trail and bleeding to death.

He rushed to her side, hoping to aid her. He looked around for her assailant who was possibly still lurking somewhere close by, hoping to finish her off.

"Hold on, please hold on," Dr. Tamimi said.

He looked in her eyes which seemed to stare into the distance. As she gasped for air, he tried holding the cut across her throat, where her windpipe had been severed.

"You'll be okay; just hold on," he said.

He lifted her in his arms, trying to show her she didn't have to be scared. As he held her in his arms, she shook; before long, she stopped moving at all. Dr. Tamimi, seeing that, said,

"No! No!"

He was saddened by what had happened to her and wished he had reached her sooner.

He sat, holding her and weeping when the police arrived. Their pistols were drawn and pointed at his head, and they yelled,

"Get on the ground!"

"I didn't do this," he said.

Tears fell down his cheeks. The police threw him to the ground violently, then beat him. After the officers decided they had assaulted him enough, they cuffed his hands behind his back and dragged him to one of the police cruisers they had left, lights blaring.

"That is my husband. He didn't do anything," his wife Mariam said, trying her best to reach him.

Among the officers was Agent Wise; he didn't hear a word Mariam said. The officers tossed the doctor into the back of a cruiser and drove him to the federal court building in Alexandria, Virginia.

When they arrived, Mr. Chantil, the lawyer appointed for Dr. Tamimi, was waiting for them. Dr. Tamimi was escorted into the interrogation room by Agent Wise and two other agents. The District Attorney was there, too, sitting across from Mr. Chantil. After taking a seat next to his lawyer, the doctor turned to the DA and asked her,

"Why am I here?"

"Besides the fact that you raped and killed that woman on the bike trail, you are here for conspiring to blow up our buildings. We have even allowed you and your people to come to this country to make better lives for yourselves when the rulers of your country would never afford you the same opportunity."

"I have not raped or killed anyone," Dr. Tamimi said, as he turned and looked at his lawyer.

"Well, we have a bloody knife with your fingerprints all over it, and we have your semen on the body of the deceased, so if you didn't rape and kill her, then you better explain how your semen got on her arm and neck."

The doctor sat there, puzzled. He tried to understand how what the DA said could be true at all. He remembered that he had been making love to his wife at the time of the incident. He said,

"I was making love to my wife when I heard a woman yelling and screaming for help. I didn't even think twice before I jumped up and went into the kitchen to get a knife. I went outside, to the trail, and I found her lying there, naked and bleeding. I tried to save her; I didn't hurt that woman at all."

"Well, she's dead, so asking her about it won't do us any good, now will it?"

The DA looked at Mr. Chantil, who hadn't said a word. The DA continued,

"Mr. Tamimi, I advise you and your lawyer to get ready for a lengthy trial."

With that, she rose, crossed the room to the door and exited.

Chapter 15

After his wife had left the visiting room, Dr. Tamimi stood and turned to leave. Then he spotted his lawyer, Marvin Miller, out of the corner of his eye. He turned around and took a seat, as Mr. Miller sat opposite and picked up the phone hanging on the wall. The doctor did likewise.

"How are you doing, Doctor?"

"I'm fine, Marvin, how may I help you?"

"Well, I promised your wife I would come by to see you yesterday but I got really busy, so I had to make it up here today. I stopped at the DA's office before coming here. I'm pleased to tell you that the rape and murder charges that were brought against you have been dismissed."

The doctor was pleased to hear that, but Marvin went on,

"However, the government has filed a super-ceding indictment charging you with being a terrorist."

Dr. Tamimi asked what that charge was based on. Marvin told him,

"Well, the government has got some guy who was facing a life sentence to say you told him to take America to war. The government has been secretly recording speeches you have made; they're trying to interpret those speeches to mean that you were promoting war against this country."

The Sheik/Dr. Tamimi shook his head, then smiled. He couldn't believe what had happened to him, but he also knew that every human being on earth was going to be tested by his Lord. No matter how much one doesn't like the test, they had no power to push it away from them.

"My country is no longer my country, you know. I looked at a map just the other day and I couldn't find Palestine anywhere on it. So much has been taken away from us, but who are we to complain?

"A Christian man blows up a building in Oklahoma City, killing hundreds of innocent people, and no one mentions the fact that he was Christian. But when a group of idiots who claim to be Muslims, do something un-Islamic, like blow up a building with a plane, all you hear about is that they were Muslim.

"The Muslims in this country are so scared to be who they are that many of them have shaved their beards and changed their beautiful names. It is not a problem for someone to know that they drink liquor, smoke, or have a girlfriend, but they are too scared to let people know that they pray five times a day, in fear of being persecuted.

"The Muslim women go without their head coverings, in fear of being beaten, insulted, raped or killed. Successful businessmen and those with brilliant minds are being locked up for giving charity.

"We as Muslims are ordered to give charity in a way that the right hand does not even know that the left hand has given. This is done so the person who is giving does not do so to show off or be seen, but we are to give strictly for the sake of the one from whom it has been given. For this, we are accused of funding terrorism."

94

The Sheik continued his comments and perspective about being Muslim in America. Next, he said,

"They hate us only because we choose to obey our Lord. We are a people who don't accept homosexuality as Jesus/Islam says. God's word, to whom peace may also be, did not accept, but for this, we are looked at as cruel people."

Marvin listened to the doctor's words and finally said,

"Doctor, I understand what you are trying to say."

But Dr. Tamimi watched as his friend removed his glasses, then replied,

"No, you don't. Allow me to finish. We are taught that this land is free. We are taught that this is the place of opportunity, but when you do as I did, and pay for your own college degree without taking a hand-out from the government; when you choose to go covered instead of partially naked; when you choose to grow your beard so that you can look like Jesus, Moses, and the rest of the humble and wise men that ever walked this earth, you are considered a terrorist.

"I understand that this is not a war against me; I know that this is a war on what I believe.

"Islam forbids drinking, smoking, fornicating, cheating, gambling, and so many other things that this country considers lawful. So, if Islam were to prevail, it would do away with the practices of this country, like the right of women to sell their bodies for money.

"Since what Islam stands for is right, and what this country stands for is wrong, then it is only right that the people destroy Islam before it destroys the life that has become so comfortable to them.

"Islam is not the problem. No! Muslims are not the problem. This is a Christian nation, and if only the Christians in this country were to force the people to abide by the laws of their Lord, then Islam wouldn't seem so strange at all; Islam and Christianity are the same in more ways than they are not.

"As our women cover to be modest, so do the nuns, but they say we are the oppressors of women. As Jesus bowed his face and prayed, so do we, but we are extremists. As long as I submit to Allah's will, I will never succumb to drinking alcohol or fornicating with women. I am not married to, neither will I cease speaking out against the people who do these things.

"Our Prophet (on whom peace may be) has said, 'Enjoin the good and forbid the evil.' Our scholars have said this means that whenever you see evil and don't speak out against it or try to change it with your hand, the evil amongst you will overpower you and become your ruler, and the prayers of the righteous will case to be answered by Allah."

Marvin listened carefully, then asked,

"Do you really think the people charging you with these acts are doing so, simply because of what you believe that is right?"

"I have done nothing but good in this country. What wrong could they possibly have to put me in prison? The truth does not set a man free in the land of those who abide by lies. We have been told by our Prophet that when Allah created Hell, he told the Angel Jabril (Gabriel) to look at it. When Jabril returned, Allah said, 'So Jabril, what do you think of it? Jabril said, 'My Lord, no one who hears about it will ever enter it if they can prevent themselves from doing so.' Allah said, 'Go back and look at it now.' Jabril returned to find the Hellfire surrounded by all the glitter and glamor that the occupants of this world are chasing. When he returned, Allah asked him, 'What do you now say?' Jabril replied, 'My Lord, no one is safe from the fire.' Then Allah said, 'Jabril, go look upon the Paradise I have created.' Jabril went and looked upon the Paradise; then he returned to Allah, who asked, 'What is it that you think of my Paradise?' Jabril said, 'My Lord, anyone who hears of it will never fail to enter it.'

"Then Allah surrounded the Paradise with the hardships in life and the tests that man does not wish to endure, to earn such a reward. He sent Jabril back to see it. When he returned, Allah asked Jabril, 'What do you say of it now?' Jabril stated, 'My Lord, no one will enter it because they will not be willing to endure the trials and tests it takes to earn such a blessing.'

The Sheik finished his story, then said to his lawyer,

"You see, Marvin, if life in prison is better for me than freedom, I choose prison, but if they put the sun in my right hand and the moon in my left, to convince me to abandon speaking out against wrongs they commit, I will never abandon telling the truth, just as my beloved Prophet did not abandon it over fourteen hundred odd years ago."

Chapter 16

After praying the *Isha* (evening prayer), Talat, Faris, Tawheed and a group of other brothers gathered in the parking lot of Dar Al Hijrah and began to talk. Talat stared towards the tree line, where Kent stood, somewhat concealed from their view. Talat asked,

"Do you think that guy right there is a CIA agent who is spying on us?"

All the brothers looked towards the wood line; once they spotted Kent, they began to give their opinions of whom or what they thought about the man who was staring. Was he spying on the mosque? If not, what was he doing there?

They had no idea of the real reason Kent had come near to Dar Al Hijrah. Kent didn't know why, himself. He didn't even know the place was a mosque, or that the woman he had been stalking had entered it. All he knew was, it was finally time for her to stop teasing him.

He had known Aza for a year; after stating his intentions to be with her physically, she continued to play hard to get. He admired her when she flaunted her body in the tight jeans and tight t-shirts she wore; the way she dressed drove him to the point of wanting her more and more. He knew that she wanted him, too, but she had played this game of hard-to-get and he was about to end it. As he stood in the trees, the brothers were still watching him. Tawheed said,

"This guy is up to no good."

He began to walk towards the parking lot where Kent stood, hidden from view; the other brothers followed behind him. Faris was walking beside Tawheed, every step of the way. He asked,

"What are you going to do?"

"I'm not sure, but I'm definitely about to tell him that he needs to find somewhere else to sight-see."

"Maybe this guy is just curious to learn about Islam," Talat said, trying to keep up with the others, who were a few steps ahead of him.

"I doubt that," Faris said.

They reached the place where the man had been standing. He had turned his back and was trying to see the side of the masjid where he saw Aza enter. Tawheed had reached him and said,

"Ay, you."

At the sound of Tawheed's voice, Kent began to reach into his coat. Tawheed reached up under his *galabiya* (long shirt) and pulled out the assault pistol. He pointed it at Kent. All the brothers stood, shocked, not knowing what to think about Tawheed having a gun.

Kent smiled and removed his hand from the inside of his coat,

102

knowing he was at a disadvantage. He turned to leave but said,

"I'll catch her fine, sexy butt later."

When he was out of sight of the brothers, they started laughing, telling Tawheed how crazy he was for what he had just done. Talat looked at the faces of the brothers who were all older than he was, and asked,

"Did you hear what that idiot just said?"

"He said something about catching her sexy butt later. What do you think he meant by that?"

Tawheed put his weapon away and said,

"He was looking at that sister who always wears those super-tight jeans; the one who goes to school with us, Talat."

"Oh, yeah, that's Aza. She dresses way too sexy."

As the group returned to the parking lot, Faris said,

"If you show a man that you have something he wants, in your pocket, your pants, or your hand, but you refuse to give it to him, he's gonna try to find a way to get it from you another way. So, what exactly do ya'll do, besides going to school and praying?"

"Well, there's nothing to do but play soccer, unless you're married," Talat said, looking at his brother Faris.

"You gonna start this stuff again?"

Faris took a seat next to Tawheed and looked at the many faces in the *halca* (circle). He said,

"Being unmarried is hard on all of the brothers, and if you think I'm lying, all you have to do is ask them."
Each brother nodded his head in agreement to what Talat had said. They all knew what it felt like to want to be with a woman but to be held back from doing so by their parents. A younger brother from Egypt and named Muhammad asked,

"So, Tawheed, are you married?"

"No, I'm not married, but I'm working on getting married, as we speak."

"So, you know what it feels like to have the burden of having to be around so many gorgeous women who are dressed provocatively every day, but not be allowed to enjoy the pleasure of them or the pleasure of a wife that can ease the desire you have to be with the opposite sex."

"I can say I know what it feels like to not be with a woman because I was locked up for eight years without being able to see, smell or hear a woman at all. I can't tell you that I have never had the pleasure to enjoy a woman and all that she has to offer."

All the brothers had given Tawheed their undivided attention, even Faris, who had also experienced the joy and blessing of being able to be married. Tawheed said,

"I grew up having sex with any woman I wanted to have sex with. In my culture, it's not wrong to fornicate. One day you have a

104

girlfriend and the next day someone else has her, and you have another. We changed our women like we changed our socks.

"This was not looked at as something dishonorable. I know women who are so good in bed that you will give them everything you value just to touch them.

"I also know women who are so fine that a man would want to marry them just to have the pleasure of saying that she is his, but this woman, who every man wants, has more than likely been with a lot of men and her image is tarnished.

"How would you feel, knowing that every man in this circle has had your wife at one point in her life?"

"I would feel embarrassed to be seen with her in public. You won't have a choice but to have her wear the full-face covering," Talat said, making the brothers laugh.

"That's what I'm trying to tell you all. Be patient, because you don't wanna marry a woman because it's just something to do. If you do that, in the end, you won't want her; you will feel like you didn't get what you really wanted; instead, you settled for her just to suppress your desires.

"A beautiful woman is a gift, but she can also be a curse, especially when she is not modest. You don't wanna have men making comments about how they would like to just give it to your wife, right there and then."

Again, the boys broke into laughter.

"I know a man can look at a sexy woman, remember what he saw, then carry that image with him to the bathroom and make love to a vision of her. I don't want nobody making love to my wife, either mentally or physically. Since men can't control their sexual desires, I'd rather have the modest woman that does attract that type of attention to herself, which may end up being a problem for her and me."

"So, what about the girl you said you have a daughter by? Is she worth marrying?" a brother asked Tawheed.

"I wouldn't marry her if she was the last woman on earth. I only wanted her because other guys had told me how good she was in bed and how easy she was to get. I never intended to get her pregnant. I never wanted her; I just wanted what she had to offer me. Now I'm stuck with her for the rest of my life. One moment of pleasure for a lifetime of pain.

"I can barely imagine what it's like for your brothers to be virgins while being surrounded by some of the sexiest, super-prettiest women in the world. I know I be masturbating like crazy or either dranking alcohol like a fish, just to keep from going insane."

Everyone laughed and stayed glued to every word he spoke, but Muhammad shook his head and said,

"It's a feeling worse than torture and what makes it even worser is know that it's billions of available good sisters out here to marry when our parents won't even let us marry them.

"As fine as the women are in this country, and you can see how sexy they are because they wear clothes that barely leave anything to the imagination, I can only imagine how the Arab and Persian women look.

"I mean, if I ever was blessed with a woman that has never been seen by the eyes or touched by the hands of another man, I would feel like I was floating on a cloud. It would be like having a world that only you knew existed."

Talat waited for a chance to speak. He said,

"You know what has been happening because of our parents not letting us get married as they have been ordered to do by Allah and his messenger?"

"No! Tell me."

Talat looked around at the other brothers as if he was seeking permission from them to reveal what it was that he was too ashamed to even think about. He looked back over to Tawheed and reluctantly said,

"Several brothers and sisters are secretly taking boyfriends and girlfriends. The brothers are dating Christian women. The sisters sneak around with disbelieving men, knowing those people will not be able to carry their sins back to the Muslim community or to their families."

With a disturbed look on his face, Tawheed asked,

"So, all of you brothers have sought permission from your parents about getting married?"

All the brothers nodded their heads in agreement.

"They always say that we need to finish school first, or they say we have to marry someone from our culture or country."

"When you go to a sister's father, seeking to marry her, he may ask you how much money you make or have in the bank. Or he'll ask how many degrees you have, and if you don't have what he thinks you should have, then he is gonna flat out tell you, no. You can't have his daughter to marry."

Muhammad shook his head and said,

"They don't even ask you how much Quran you have memorized or how many people will bear witness that your good outweighs your bad."

Tawheed could not believe what he was hearing. He thought to himself, *it's no wonder that the sisters were sneaking around with disbelieving men.*

There were already forty women to every man, which had been statistically proved, but now a sister had to worry about all of the brothers who were available, except her father wouldn't allow her to marry. Tawheed began to think about the many incarcerated men he had met. With those men in prison, the number of good eligible men is even higher.

There also were a lot of homosexuals who had no intention of being with a woman. Then there were a number of men being killed in the streets, or at war, every single day. How was one to hope for good when all odds, including their parents, were against them?

The brother named Harun said as he wiped the sweat from his hands on his shirt,

"I've thought about leaving this country to go back to Oman. I know if I don't get married soon, I'll never keep from fornicating, especially when women who are dressed still appear to be naked."

"This has been prophesied by our Prophet, Salla la hu alai wa salaam (on whom may peace be upon)."

"I could see if it was as simple as lowering your gaze, but not here. No! If you look away from this woman, then you'll see the next woman dressed just as sexy," Talat said, then he added,

"I often think the only way to lower your gaze is by walking around with a blindfold on!"

The others laughed, and Talat went on,

"Man, I ain't about to go through all of that. Ima just keep looking at all of them until I go blind."

That made the brothers laugh.

"Our scholars have agreed that it's best to masturbate whenever you feel as if you can't restrain yourself from fornicating."

"Yeah, but after a while, even masturbating won't quench your thirst or desire to be with a woman."

"What are you gonna do when you run across a female like Dawn, my daughter's mother," Tawheed asked.

Faris, who had spent the time just soaking up all that he was hearing asked,

"What do you mean by that, brother?"

"I mean, you have some women who aren't willing to hear you tell them you won't do what they want you to do to them. Aggressive women who, if given the chance and the right place, rape you straight up."

The brothers were laughing so hard that some of them fell to the ground. Tawheed continued,

"Sex is a wonderful thing, but that great pleasure can also bring about a lifetime of misery, like AIDS or a baby by a woman you can't stand at all.

"The only time that me and Dawn are able to get along to the point where we are not arguing is when we are having sex. The rest of the time we are arguing about nothing at all, or saying things to try to hurt each other, or make one another jealous."

"Have you ever asked her to take her *shahadah* (testimony of faith)," a brother asked.

"Yeah, I've asked her plenty of times, and if she would have, I would have married her without thinking about it twice. There's something you brothers will never truly understand because the women you all are seeking, and the women you know, have an Islamic background. But if I married Dawn without her becoming Muslim, she would have my daughter thinking that it's okay to wear tight clothes.

"Dawn would have her celebrating Christmas and every other holiday that we Muslims don't celebrate."

One of the brothers asked Tawheed,

"Why can't you just let her have it her way sometimes and you have it yours sometimes. I mean, wouldn't it work out between you and her if you choose to compromise a little?"

"There can be no compromise in Islam," Tawheed answered. "Have you not seen where Allah tells his prophet that the Jews and the Christians of his time won't be pleased with him until he chooses to compromise with them, having them practice their religion one day, in exchange for them following his religion?"

"Yeah, I read that," Faris said, smiling.

One of the brothers said,

"Once you start compromising, you open yourself up to

continued compromise and then when you do decide to put your foot down, they will never take you seriously."

"Exactly," Tawheed said, looking at the other brother. "Let's say I did compromise with her and believe me, I once tried to make a compromise, and it didn't work. But let's say I did.

"Here's what's likely to happen. She and I were at a carry out once. I was standing outside talking on my cell phone as she stood in the store, ordering our food. A group of guys walked past, and when they seen the way her booty and hips looked in the tight jeans she was wearing, they stopped in their tracks.

"One of the men started saying how he would taste her and touch her and this and that until he went too far. He went inside the store and tried to talk to her, and when I said something to him, he acted as if he wanted to kill me."

Tawheed recalled one other example,

"Another time, I let her trick me into staying in the bed with her for a few minutes, knowing it was time for me to pray. Before long, we started messing around and had sex. The time had flown by, and when I looked at the clock, I noticed that I had to make up not one but two prayers.

"I used to take her around my male cousins, who all used to be staring at her booty and chest. They all wanted to have sex with her. While she was around, they wouldn't dare take their eyes off her. They used to tell each other about wanting to have sex with her and when I found out, I couldn't be mad.

"I used to think that since she had given herself to me so easy, that she must have been cheating one me as well. When I confronted her about it, she said, 'We're not married, so I can have sex with whoever I want to have sex with.'

"She mentioned something about her being Christian and how the Bible said for her to be married, so in her eyes, and in the eyes of God, if she was sleeping with me, or some other guy, it was still seen as her fornicating."
One of the brothers asked,

"Do disbelieving women perform *Istinja* (proper purification after using the restroom)?"

"No, they don't know nothing about that, just as many disbelieving men don't.

"I used to urinate standing up, not having any idea that all of my urine was hitting the water in the toilet and jumping back onto my legs. I never thought about using water with the toilet paper I wiped with. It took for a brother who was a Muslim to ask me if I had wanted a clean shirt or a rag, wouldn't I use water and soap to clean it.

"All my life I had been just wiping and getting up, so no, the disbelieving women do not wipe themselves properly, so they have filth all over them when they get up from the toilet, just as most men do after they get up from it as well."

Another brother asked Tawheed,

"Does your baby mother get mad at you for looking at other women, when she herself is dressing in a way that causes other men to look at her the same way, or think about her in the same way?"

"She definitely gets mad when she catches me staring at some other woman, but when I get mad at a man for looking at her, she says, 'You can't stop people from looking at me.' It's a double-edged sword."

A brother named Isa asked Tawheed,

"So, what do you do when she gets mad at you for looking at another woman?"

"I turned around and pointed to the twelve men who were all eating her alive with their eyes at the carry out; that was something she enjoyed," Tawheed answered.

"Like I said, I can't take her anywhere or introduce her to anyone because all they think about when they see her is having sex with her.

"Now, if ya'll think that having sex with any random woman, just to quench your urge, is worth going through all of that, then be my guest.

"Matter of fact, I'll let ya'll have Dawn, and if ya'll got some money, I'm sure she'll let ya'll have her,"
Tawheed said, making everyone laugh. He added,

"Nah, but all jokes aside, we are all Muslims, and none of us can change the laws that Allah has sent down to us to be followed.

"If your fathers aren't giving you your rights, you still have the option to go to an Islamic judge who will either make him give you your rights or strip him of his rights over you in the matter. It's better to get married and have your family mad at you than to be sitting in hellfire because you made Allah mad at you."

Chapter 17

It took less than three weeks for a jury of twelve to find Doctor Tamimi guilty of treason and conspiring to declare war against the United States of America.

Four months later, he was sentenced to life plus seventy years, to make sure that even if the conviction were overturned on appeal, he would do at least twenty years of the seventy years before he was out of jail and free.

Along with forty or more prisoners, he entered the R and D part of Alexandria Jail before being transferred to Hazelton Federal Prison to serve his time.

"You all get naked and put on these," one of the deputy marshals said, holding up a stack of light blue paper jumpsuits.

Without shame, all the other men removed all of their clothes and stood next to each other, naked as the day they were born. The doctor, who hadn't ever allowed anyone except his wife to see him naked, hesitated to undress. One of the marshals yelled and made a threatening gesture at him.

He had to comply with what he was told. After getting dressed in the paper jumpsuit, which made him feel as if he was going to break out, he followed the line to another marshal, who placed shackles on his ankles.

After that, he continued down the line until he reached another marshal who placed a chain around his waist that connected to the handcuffs placed around each wrist.

In a single-file line, he and all the others boarded a bus that would soon take them to the federal hold over in Northern Neck, in Warsaw County, Virginia. It took more than six hours to reach Northern Neck, but none of the men on the bus complained; they knew the long ride would be their last chance for decades to see the outside world.

When they arrived at Northern Neck, the doctor was taken to a part of the jail that was secluded.

"Take off that blue suit after you step into the cell," a guard told him as he unlocked the huge metal cell door so Dr. Tamimi could enter.

The Sheikh stepped into the cell where the floor was flooded with water. He took off the jumpsuit and handed it to the guard who was watching.

"This cell is flooded with water, sir," the doctor said, trying to stand on tiptoes in the paper-soled shoes they had given him.

"I know. Go ahead and take those shoes off, as well, and I'll get you some new ones," the guard said.

The guard waited for the doctor to hand him all his articles of clothing. Once that was done, the guard said,

"Bend over and spread your cheeks."

The doctor complied, although he felt embarrassed to do so.

"Now lift up your nuts and cough."

Again, he did what he was told to do. The two guards seemed to enjoy seeing him naked; they laughed to one another. Then, one of the guards closed the cell door and locked it. At that, the doctor said,

"Sir, you forgot to give me the clothes."

A guard opened the slot in the door that was used to pass food to the prisoners and said,

"First come over here and let me cuff your hands behind your back."

Again, the doctor did as he was told. When the slot closed again, he turned and faced the small glass window in the middle of the door. The guard began to laugh, but the doctor said,

"Sir, I need some clothes; it's freezing in this cell."

He looked at the air vent; icy cold air blew in powerfully.

"Tell Bin Laden to get you some clothes, you terrorist piece of junk," the guard said.

He turned and walked away from the door. It would be more than three hours before another guard came down that hall to check on the inmates on that tier. The Sheikh, who was a diabetic, lay across the metal bed frame, shaking. He had begun to hyperventilate, as well. He had tried to move several times, but each time he did the handcuffs on his wrists tightened, cutting deeper into his flesh and making him bleed.

Unable to pray and feeling as if he was about to die at any moment, the Sheikh continued to remember Allah, knowing it wouldn't be long before he would be a step closer to his Lord. He closed his eyes as he felt himself losing consciousness.

It was just then that a lieutenant, who had just happened to be making a random stop on the tier, noticed him lying naked with the cuffs on his wrists. He made an emergency medical call on his radio, then he opened the cell door and rushed to the doctor. He removed the handcuffs then tried to stop the bleeding from his wrists with a dirty piece of a sheet; it was the only thing left in the cell.

The medical staff rushed into the cell. They put the doctor on their stretcher and tried to bring him back to life.

Chapter 18

More than what appeared to be at least one million people stood on the Mall in DC for a remake of the Nation of Islam's Million Man March. As he had always done, Kent showed up, dressed to impress and knowing that many beautiful women would be everywhere in the city then.

He passed through the huge crowd of clean-shaven, bald-headed black men and snickered to himself, *So much power and so conscious of self, but still not even able to afford your own country.*

He continued walking towards a beautiful woman he had spotted from a distance. As he traveled through the sea of black people, who looked at him as if he was crazy, he thought about the fact that inside, he was blacker than they would ever be.

His attention on the woman was diverted when a man with a long gray beard and a Kifia scarf wrapped around his head began to shout. He was saying something about what was in the Quran and how the men that were in the Nation of Islam were not Muslim at all.

"You people are not teaching Islam; you are teaching hate and culturalism, which is not something found inside the very book that you yourselves have claimed to be the message of Allah."

He continued proclaiming, even shouting at the top of his voice,

"*Surah* (chapter) five, *ayat* (verse) three tells us that Allah has perfected our religion, so this which you are doing is new and what is invented. This and you will be tossed into the fire."

With his right hand, he waved the Quran above his head and said,

"Allah says in *surah* sixteen, *ayat* forty-four, that he has sent this Quran to Muhammad, who died over fourteen hundred years ago. Only he will be in charge of explaining it to us, not your so-called prophets who are not prophets at all, but hypocrites.

"We are told by our Prophet to grow the beard to distinguish ourselves from the woman and to show the trait of the prophets, but here, you are cutting your beards so that you can imitate the women of this culture, instead of its men.

"You stand against homosexuality, but you molest your faces to look just like the homosexuals."

The men closest to the speaker must have become frustrated by what he was saying; before he could get another word out of his mouth, the man and other men had him in a headlock down on the ground. They were stomping him.

Kent, who wasn't at all interested in aiding the man whom he thought, brought the trouble on himself, tried to pass, but when he did, one of the men grabbed him. Kent pulled out his gun and smacked the man with it. When the other men tried to subdue him, Kent began firing shots.

Before long, he found he was out of bullets and began running through the crowd to escape. As he stepped out into the street, an under-cover police officer opened fire on him, plugging him twice in his shoulder and arm. He was placed under arrest and taken to the hospital.

Chapter 19

It had been nearly a year since he got out of prison and Tawheed had finally seen the blessings that, at first, he never thought would fall into his lap in abundance. He bypassed getting an apartment and instead bought a house. He gained custody of his daughter from Dawn, who was more concerned with trying to ditch the girl off on him so she could run around and live her life.

He had two cars and more than enough money in the bank to take a wife. Although he had disobeyed Allah by committing some of the greater sins, Allah still blessed him with everything his heart had desired, and more.

As he sat in the threshold of her door, watching her get dressed, Tawheed nearly cried at the site of his beautiful little girl. She stood in front of the mirror, covered from head to toe.

"Hurry, baby," he said, smiling.

He left the doorway and went to the living room. He could feel his heart pounding away in his chest as he sat and thought about meeting Tawheeda, the sister of Muhammad, his friend from Egypt.

Today would be the first of many chaperoned days that he and she would have. Her brother and father were present, and that would allow them to get to know each other, to see if they were at all compatible and wanted to marry.

Finally, he had received everything he had prayed for, and he was well-pleased with his Lord. He looked forward to getting to know Tawheedah for who she was, instead of trying only to see what she looked like.

All the relationships he had in his past were based on physical attraction, which kept him from ever getting to know the women he had pursued. This time it would be different; this time, things would end right, because they would start right.

Chapter 20

Kent, who had been found guilty of discharging a firearm into a crowd on federal property, was sentenced to five years, which was the mandatory minimum one could receive for catching a federal gun charge. The fact that he would be off the streets for fifty months or better didn't bother him at all.

His transfer from Peterburg Federal Holding to Atlanta gave him no idea of what he would be facing when he reached Hazelton United States Prison, the deadliest federal penitentiary in the nation.

None of that bothered him at all, not even the fact that the white boys he didn't have any intention of rolling with, would soon pressure him into choosing to roll with them, or fall victim to what they intended to do to him for not rolling.

As Kent arrived in Oklahoma, Sheikh Tamimi arrived on the compound in Hazelton. He wore the beige jumpsuit he had been given. As he walked, he was greeted by *Salaamu Alaikum* from more than twelve other Muslims who knew, weeks in advance, he was coming there.

"*Wa Alaikum Salaam Wa Rahma tullahi,*" he said with a smile, as Sunni and Luqman made their way to him.

"Take his bags to his building," Sunni said.

He looked at two other brothers whose names were Shaheed and Qareem. The brothers grabbed the bags from the Sheikh and walked towards his building. He stood with a puzzled look on his face, wondering how they even knew where he was going to be living.

Prison was a funny world; the prisoners were the ones who lived inside its walls. That made it natural for them to have knowledge of everything that went on inside those walls.

Besides the doctor, no man within the prison had been locked up for preaching Islam, so the rules changed from the way they were played in the real world. Men had to be checked, and those in charge of such men usually ruled over them with iron fists.

"Come walk with us, brother, we wanna talk to you about a few things," Luqman said, as the three of them headed down the walkway in the direction of the rec yard.

"We are knowledgeable about Islam, based on the books we have read and memorized but none of us have learned the *Deen* (way of life) at the feet of the scholars as it is properly taught, so our understanding, compared to yours, is insignificant," Luqman said.

"As you know from being a college professor and student of knowledge, a thousand people can read the same book, and each of them can come up with a different understanding of what it is they have read or thought they read."

"This is the reason why, in a class setting, students aren't just given books to read and left on their own to interpret them, based on their own understanding.

136

"In college, they have professors to explain to the students what they've read, and in Islam, we have our rightly-guided *Salaf u Saleeheen* (predecessors).

"As we all know, whenever anything of the Quran was revealed, the Prophet *Salalahu alaihi wa salaam* (whom may peace be upon) would ask his companions, 'What did Allah mean by this?'

"These people who were the best of us and better than we would say, 'Allah and his messenger know best.'

"Our beloved Prophet would then tell them what Allah meant by what it was he had revealed to them, and this is called the *tafsir* (explanation)."

Luqman, Sunni, and the Sheikh continued walking. Luqman said to the older man,

"Everybody's explanation is not sufficient. If we are uncertain of the explanation that has been given by our beloved Prophet, then we remain silent. It is left to those who know to tell us what it means, and I don't mean leaving it up to just anyone, like a guy who has studied on his own in prison for fifty years, even if he has memorized thousands of books."

Luqman continued speaking to the Sheikh,

"This is why we feel you should take the place as the Imam here at the prison. You have been confirmed by the proper sources to be qualified to teach in various arts, while none of us have. You also have memorized the whole of the Quran, with its proper interpretation."

Doctor Tamimi paused a moment and thought carefully about what Luqman had said and had requested.

"I would love to help you brothers in any way that I can, and I shall do just that as long as I am here *Insha Allah* (if Allah wills). But you must understand that the only reason the administration agreed to even let me out of the hole where I just was, on twenty-three-hour lockdown, was under the conditions that I don't take the position as Imam."

"I had no knowledge of that," Luqman said, "but I was asked by the captain if it was okay to let you on the yard."

The Sheikh looked at him, disturbed, as he absorbed what it was he had just heard. Luqman continued,

"See, brother, this is prison and prison is a dangerous place. We had received word that some Aryan brothers, who are a vicious group of racist white men, were plotting to stab and kill you for blowing up the World Trade Center."

"I'm not even in here for doing that," the Sheikh replied.

"Yeah, I know and they know, as well, that had they touched you, it would be an all-out war that they would lose instantly."

138

Luqman was glad that subject was raised and said they had a meeting to attend on the baseball diamond. The three men began walking in that direction.

When they arrived, the two hundred plus brothers who were waiting for them gave the greeting of peace, and the three newcomers returned it.

"*Inna humdulillah wa salaaut wa salaamu wa ala rasoolulah wa ala allihi wa sabiyeen ilah yamuden,* (all praises are due to Allah and may blessing be upon him and his companions until the day of judgement."

Having finished the exchange of greeting, Luqman asked,

"First of all, are there any problems or concerns that need to be addressed in the community?"

"Yeah," an enormous brown-skinned brother that had a long scar on his left cheek said, looking at Luqman.

"What is it, Wadi?"

"Well, last week Safeeq got off the bus, and his DC homies were asking him to see his paperwork. They are of the belief that he is a confidential informant who has not just worked for the government at one time, but who is still working for them."

Wadi continued telling Luqman and the brothers,

"They say that one of the guys that he put in prison is here and he is saying that he has two weeks to get off of the yard or produce his paperwork, showing that he does not work for the government, or they are going to kill him."

Luqman considered what Wadi had reported, then replied,

"This issue is a very sensitive one, no doubt. This issue has broken up many communities within the prison system because nearly every man in here has been snitched on, and as a result of that, they have lost everything they love, including their freedom.

"This is prison, and within these walls, men are being killed, extorted, raped…and drugs of all kinds are being sold.

"This alone means no one wants anyone who has told on their cases to be around them at all, which I understand. It is my belief that the brother, if found guilty of having snitched on someone on this compound, should be checked into the hole and transferred from this prison.

"If not that, then a lot of men will be killed trying to defend a man who will more than likely tell on them, once they do whatever it is they have to do to defend his life."

Sunni turned and looked at the Sheikh, then said,

"Brother, do you have anything to add to this?"

The Sheikh replied,

"Well, yes. First, we are not gangsters, and even though we reside in a world of criminals, we must not pick up their thinking patterns or behavior patterns.

"Whenever we are faced with a situation, we always refer it back to Allah and his messenger. We must not use our own analysis of reason because whatever occurs based on our decisions, we will, no doubt, be held accountable for, in the sight of Allah."

With frustration in his voice, Wadi asked,

"So, what are we to do? Let some weak back snitch cause the whole community to go to war trying to defend him from the very people he has wronged, just so he can turn around and tell on us, too, once we kill men in order to protect him?"

The Sheikh considered the question and replied,

"What has to be done is we have to do whatever it is that Allah and his Messenger have ordered us to do and that requires *hikman* (wisdom). First, we ascertain the truth, to see if what is being said is even true. Next, we must understand that, no matter what, once a man becomes a Muslim, Allah has forgiven him of all his past sins. So, who are we to continue to judge him for what his Lord, our Lord, has forgiven him for?

"We must also realize that a Muslim's blood and property are sacred, and there are only three reasons why Muslim blood can be spilled: If he has apostatized from Islam; if he has killed someone and they wish to have his life be taken in return; and if he is found guilty of committing adultery."

141

The Sheikh paused a moment, seeing the brothers thinking over what he had said. Then he continued,

"Snitching is not punishable by death in our way of life. Whenever those who fought against our prophet and his companions lost a man or woman, the Muslims did not send that person back to them to be slaughtered."

"As I said," the Sheikh continued, "we must refer all information back to Allah and his messenger; we must realize that if we do place this man in the hole, we are taking the position of those who choose to oppress him…and if we are not careful, we will do more harm than good."

Everyone in the circle was speechless. In their hearts, they all thought they knew what to do, but now they were confused, as if at once the choice hadn't been clear. A brother named Rafeek said,

"I have a question, as well, Imam."

"Well speak, Rafeek."

"I see a lot of Spanish guys interested in Islam, but the gangs they role with like the piasas and suranyos threaten to kill them if they leave their gangs to become Muslim. What should they do? And if they do become Muslim, and they have to be defended for their choice to be Muslim, what do we do?"

Luqman said to Rafeek,

"As you just heard the Sheikh say, a Muslim's blood is sacred, and they cannot be turned back by us, over to those people."

Another brother said,

"I got a question. My name is Mujahid, and I just got off the bus. Since being here, a brother in my block has come to me several times, asking me if I'm okay. I'm not sure what's the problem with the brother. Maybe he thinks I'm a snitch or something, but him constantly coming to ask me if I'm okay is starting to irritate me."

Raising his hand to be recognized, a brother named Bilal said,

"I'm the brother in his dorm who he is talking about."

Luqman turned to Mujahid and said,

"In three days, seven people have been killed on this compound. Helicopters are landing on the yard like there's an air pad in the middle of it.

"The ABs have been at war with the DC guys, and just last month, the Dirty White Boys got into it with the piasas. The brother understands how quickly something can happen, so we check on each other constantly, to ensure that none of us is in danger, and if so, we can handle it before it gets out of hand.

"Just last month, a brother had brushed shoulders with an Aryan Brotherhood and even though they both had said, 'excuse me,' and that they were sorry, the ABs ended up killing the brother

143

later on that day. So, when a brother asks you if you are okay, just be grateful that he is checking on you.

"I know that you're new here, Mujahid, but Bilal is on the security staff, and it is his job to check to make sure that the brothers in his block are okay at all times."

Sunni looked around at the faces of all the brothers and asked,

"Anything else that needs to be addressed?"

When no one else said anything, he said a short supplication in Arabic, closing the meeting.

Chapter 21

It took all of six weeks for Kent to make it out of Oklahoma Transit Center back to West Virginia and he was becoming more frustrated with each day. He was mad as hell about the whole process of having to go all the way to Oklahoma City and catch a plane all the way back around the country to get to West Virginia from Atlanta's hold-over.

If Oklahoma-TC was a glimpse of what he was to expect at Hazelton USP, then he knew he needed a knife just as soon as he got off the bus. If he hadn't noticed anything else, he had noticed how the Spanish wouldn't be cellmates with blacks, and how whites seemed to all be in gangs based on their race.

As the bus pulled up to Hazelton USP, for the first time he would be incarcerated, and Kent began to feel nervous.

"Alright, listen up for your names," yelled one of the marshals standing at the front of the bus in front of the steel gate.

He looked down at the clipboard in his hands. As he called their names, each man whose name was called reluctantly stood up from his seat and moved up the aisle to the marshal. The look on each of their faces told a story of its own.

All the tough guys realized they were going to a place where it didn't matter who you were, how much money you had, or how many men you killed. Prison was a place where a man who was nothing on the streets could be a man who stood above all other men. Unlike the real world, there was nothing in prison to give a man instant gratification.

Even the billionaires wore simple beige shirts and pants. Everyone was allowed only three hundred minutes a month, and everyone could only spend the limit of three hundred twenty dollars, which meant, no matter how much money you might have been worth, it could not sway anything in your favor in prison.

The worst of the men on the streets found themselves being either humbled or killed, once they ended up in prison. He, too, would come to learn about this very soon.

Once his name was called, Kent moved up the aisle to the exit of the bus. The correctional officer said,

"Alright, listen up! We know that a lot of you are tough guys and killers but in here, that means nothing and you'll come to know that soon and all too well.

"I advise you to get yourselves a knife as soon as you can, and if you have told on someone, or have killed someone's people who might be on this yard, the SHU (Special Housing Unit) is that way."

The officer pointed to the SHU on the left, then continued,

"Me and my co-workers will not try to stop a gang of men from stabbing you to death, so be smart. We only make eighty grand a year. Trust me; it's not even close to enough to take a knife in the chest for."

When he finished speaking, over half the men who got off the bus were taken to protective custody. It was not because all of them were scared. Many of the men were in gangs that couldn't walk the yard; they knew if they tried to walk, they would be murdered instantly.

Others had killed family members of men they knew were on the yard. Without having a knife, they knew they were at a clear disadvantage.

"Okay, now for the rest of you who choose to go to the yard, follow me," the officer said.

In a single-file line, Kent and the rest of the twenty or so other men walked through a doorway and into the United States' deadliest penitentiary.

"So, who are you gonna roll with, the white boys or your homies from DC," a black inmate who had also been in Petersburg holding with him asked Kent.

"I'm a man. I don't need nobody to help me do nothing. Cowards roll in packs, and I'm a lion, I roll over packs."

"Yeah, evidently, you've never been to the penitentiary," the black inmate said, turning around to face front again. Then he said to Kent,

"The best of killers have been killed by the simplest quiet men in places like this."

"Yeah, we'll see," Kent said.

He began focusing on the walls that surrounded the place. Another inmate who was behind him said,

"If it's not flying, you'll never see it. This is the place where men really find out how strong they are mentally and physically."

Chapter 22

Once he was inside the main compound of the prison, Kent realized he was in a world of trouble. Groups of men with tattoos all over their bodies and faces stood in regiments divided by race; they did calisthenics that even most Marines would be unable to do. First, the man in the front of the group went down; once he finished, the others followed his lead. Most of the men had arms as wide as the ones on offensive linemen in the NFL.

Without making eye contact, Kent traveled up the corridor, which was gated off from the rest of the yard. He continued walking to his designated building. Once he reached his cellblock, he went to the assigned cell and placed his bag on the floor.
Two huge white men with bald heads and tattoos all over their bodies went into the cell behind him and closed the door.

He backed against the wall and got in a stance, which let the two men know he was ready to fight. Both men laughed and reached into their shirts. They pulled out metal lawnmower blades sharpened into swords. That did not cause Kent to flinch at all.

"Either you can get on board with what it is we're doing here, or you can die right there where you stand," one of the men said, staring into Kent's eyes.

"Ya'll gonna have to kill me, cause I ain't about to submit to no "men" while I'm breathing."

153

"Look, homie, you're white, and the whites roll with the whites around here, so it wouldn't even be wise of you to go to war with us.

"None of these other groups are gonna have your back, which means you'll have problems you will never be able to handle on your own."

"I'll pass," Kent said.

He thought about how he would get the swords from the men, then kill them with their own weapons.

Just as the two ABs were about to rush Kent, the door opened. The commotion from outside the cell made the two white men turn to see a mob of Muslims standing around the door and out-numbering the group of white boys watching the cell, so the two ABs inside could handle their business.

"This cell here is a Muslim cell, Brudda, so whatever beef ya'll got with this man is gonna have to wait," Luqman said, getting up in the face of the bigger of the two ABs that had moved back outside the cell.

"Thanks, I didn't need nobody to come to my aid," Kent said, staring Luqman in the eyes.

"We aren't here to save you, white boy," Luqman said.

As he spoke, three more Muslims entered the cell and went past Kent. They went to the locker, and after tugging away at it, they managed to pull it off the wall, revealing a huge hole behind it. Saddiq reached into the hole and retrieved two bags that he handed to Luqman.

Luqman untied one bag and looked inside. After he was satisfied that what they had come to get was still in the bags, he reached into his waist and removed a knife from his hip. Kent stood still and wondered what was to come next. Then Luqman dropped the knife on the bed and left the cell; the other brothers followed him.

Sadiq, who was the last to leave the cell, turned to Kent and asked,

"Where are you from?"

"I'm from DC."

"Well, you better get with your homies quick because the next time you see them white boys we just ran out of the cell, they're gonna be trying to kill you, or worse."

Sadiq also told Kent,

"I advise you to keep that knife on you at all times. And if you are around for me to see you again, you need to realize that even the toughest man in prison can easily fall victim to a bunch of hyenas."

Chapter 23

More than a month had passed since they both arrived at USP Hazelton. Only one of them was content with his life as it was, while the other one, Kent, who had felt at first that prison would be a cakewalk for him, now realized he was facing the most challenging situation of his life.

The Sheikh was grateful to Allah for allowing him to have the time to focus on reading more Quran. He knew if his enemies were to martyr him, he would receive Paradise; if they kept him locked up for the rest of his life, they would give him all the opportunity and time he needed to prepare himself to meet his Lord on that inevitable day of judgment.

As he sat and ate his food, he looked towards Kent, who was not at all comfortable having to sit with his homies from DC. He had been forced to choose a group or die, but it didn't sit well with him. He wanted to kill the men who had foolishly tried to make him join them, but he knew that would be a suicide mission, at the least.

As he rose from his seat at the DC table, he walked past the six tables where the Muslims ate. Once he reached the last of their tables, he stopped in his tracks, turning to face the Sheikh.

"What is the difference between the people who are in the Nation of Islam and you brothers?"

Each brother at that table had puzzled looks on their faces. They stared at him, shocked by the question he asked them. The Sheikh smiled, then stood up. He turned to the brothers and said,

"I'll answer the question for him."

Speaking to Kent, the Sheikh said,

"Now, if you have a moment, you and I can make a few laps around the rec yard, and I'll explain this to you."

He and Kent walked across the kitchen and toward the tray room, where they discarded their trays. They left the kitchen, passed the compound, and went into the rec yard. Kent asked,

"Do Muslims really believe that all white people are devils?"

"No, Muslims don't but those who call themselves Muslims and who are in the Nation of Islam, do believe this."

The Sheikh continued,

"First, before I answer your question or talk in depth about what the Nation of Islam does and does not believe, I will clarify to you what it is that we, as Muslims, do believe.

"We have five pillars which hold this belief system of ours together. We also have six articles of faith. The five pillars are: first, *La ilaha ilallah Muhmmadar Rasooluia*, which means "there is no god but Allah and Muhammad is his messenger;" second, we must pray the five prayers every day; third, we must fast for the month of Ramadan; fourth, we must pay a tax on our wealth in order for the poor to be taken care of; and fifth, if we are able, we must go visit the house of Allah, which is the *Kaaba*, at least once in our lifetimes."

The Sheikh explained that the *Kaaba* was in the middle of the most sacred mosque in Islam. Then he began to explain more to Kent,

"The six articles of our faith are as follows: first, we believe in Allah as the only God; second, we believe in his angels; third, we believe in all of his messengers; fourth, we believe in all of the books Allah sent down to our Prophet and his other prophets and messengers; fifth, we believe in pre-ordainment, the good and the bad of it; and sixth, we believe in the day of judgment.

"The Nation of Islam dis-believes in the very thing that makes us Muslims in the first place, which is that there is no other God than Allah. They believe that a man is an incarnation of God, which does not just take one out of the fold of Islam, but it also labels you as a dis-believer.

"Second, they don't believe that Muhammad is the prophet of Islam and was the last prophet and messenger sent by Allah to mankind."

Kent had been listening closely to the Sheikh, and asked,

"So, you're saying that the people with the bald heads and clean-shaven faces, who be selling bean pie's, are not even Muslim?"

The Sheikh replied,

"Exactly, they're not even Muslim."

"So Muslims believe in Jesus?"

"Of course, we believe in Jesus (whom may peace be upon). Remember I told you that we believe in all of Allah's messengers and prophets, if, in fact, it is proved that they were that. Jesus has been confirmed to us through the Quran. If you pay close attention, you will see that the Muslims follow Jesus' ways, more so than Christians do."

Kent questioned the Sheikh further,

"If God is a good God, then why does he allow innocent children, who have done no wrong at all, to die?"

The Sheikh replied,

"We have no idea why Allah allows whatever he allows to happen. We are so quick to try to tell the creator what he can do with what he created as if we know what is best for them. He is all knowing, so whatever he does is sufficient."

"But why would he take the life of a child who has harmed no man," Kent asked.

He stopped in his tracks; his eyes began to tear up. The Sheikh paused with him, then said,

"We have no knowledge of the unseen, and we have no knowledge of this world or ourselves, except what it is that our Creator has taught us. Here we are trying to figure out why he does what he does when we aren't even able to figure out why, at times, we do what it is that we do ourselves.

"We do not thank him for the time he has allowed for us to be in the lives of those we love; instead, we complain when he chooses to take them out of our lives. A Muslim is one who submits his will to the creator. Islam is a life of submission. Once we understand who Allah the Creator is, and what position we play in all of this, we will not complain about death or about all life's mis-happenings, but instead, we say *Al hamdu lillah* (All praise be to Allah), for the good and the bad.

"If you and I were blessed to live forever, we would end up being miserable, because we would out-live everyone we loved. We would have to watch endlessly, as everything we love and cherish, dies off, again and again. If every man was blessed to get what he prayed for, and I was praying for my wife, and you were praying for my wife, who would end up getting her? More than likely, if we both got her, neither of us would want her anymore.

"We have no idea why our hearts skip a beat and when our scrotum sacks shrink up in the winter or expand in the summer. We as people are not in control of this, and most of us have no idea why this even occurs. Sperm must stay at a certain temperature or die.

163

But are we keeping all the functions of our bodies in line, or is he who created us doing it?"

Kent wiped the tears from his eyes as he looked at the Sheikh,

"I grew up very poor, me and my little brother and mother. We didn't have anything, and after suffering poverty, God comes along and takes the life of the only thing I ever loved. There comes the point where life is more harmful to a person than death; it also is proven that money can be a bigger curse than poverty."

The Sheikh listened thoughtfully, then he replied,

"Maybe Allah took your brother to get your attention. If he can take the life of an innocent child who has done no wrong, then you should know that he can and will take your life for being disobedient to him.

"Pay attention to the signs. People are being snatched off this earth every single day. Who is to say that you and I are not next? Instead of being angry at Allah for his choice to bring back to himself that which was his from the start, ponder about who he is and what your role is in this vast cycle called life.

"I can see that you are hurt, based on your loss, but we all lose people and things. When we die, everything on this earth that we have gathered up and amassed will be left behind. All you will take with you is your good and bad deeds."

Kent remained silent, but he had heard every word the Sheikh said. Then the Sheikh continued,

"I will give you some books to read because the better you understand a thing, the greater you'll be able to comprehend what it is that you are up against in this world. Now, if you are not doing anything, follow me to my dorm, and I'll get the two books for you."

Kent followed the Sheikh, and when they reached the building, they went inside heading straight for the cell. Once inside, the Sheikh went to his cabinet and took down two books, *What Did Jesus Really Say*, and the Quran. Kent looked around the well-kept cell that seemed to blossom a very pleasurable scent. Then he asked,

"Who lives in here with you?"

"No one," the Sheikh said, handing the two books to Kent.

"There's this thing about whites only bunking with whites and blacks with blacks around here," Kent said, leaning against the wall as his eyes met the floor.

"I wouldn't know about that because there is no racism in Islam at all, so the Muslims bunk with anyone," the Sheikh said.

"Allah is concerned with the soul of the man and the quality of what's in his heart, not the color of his skin," he said. "If you'd like, you can move into this cell with me, as long as you're not smoking and drinking or doing other things what will interrupt my peaceful way of living."

165

Kent couldn't believe what he just heard. He told the Sheikh,

"Yeah, I don't smoke or drink anymore. I was completely wild on the streets, but I see that all of the animals are in here, in this cage. If I'm not careful, Ima end up getting killed, or having to kill someone, which will leave me stuck in here forever."

"Yes, I feel good about your moving into this cell, as long as you are alright with me praying five times a day," the Sheikh said, smiling.

Chapter 24

As soon as Kent could gather his belongings from his old cell, he moved into the cell with the Sheikh; he spent most of his time with the older man.

He spent so much time with the Sheikh that the other Muslims started getting jealous of their relationship. But some had questions.

"Ay, Sheikh, why do you keep allowing for this disbeliever to hang around you all the time," Hakee asked, as he rose to his feet after ending a set of pushups.

"Why would I allow for him to be around me," the Sheikh repeated Hakee's question, with a puzzled look on his face.

"He's not Muslim, plus, he's white, so he should go and hang around his own people."

"Were you always a Muslim, Hakee?"

"Naw, I took my *shahadah* about four years ago," Hakee said, before dropping back down to do more pushups.

"If we who possess the Truth do not mingle with those who have no knowledge of what we know, then how will anyone ever know about Islam at all? And how would you have found out about Islam?"

Hakee hadn't thought about what the Sheikh said; he remained quite unable to answer the questions. The Sheikh looked at Kent, who was on the basketball court not far from him.

He crossed to Kent, who asked,

"What's up? I see your Muslim brothers don't like it when I

hang with you."

"That's not at all true. Do you have a moment?"

"Yeah, what's up?"

"Well, come on, let's walk and talk."

The Sheikh and Kent continued walking toward the track and began to talk. The Sheikh asked,

"So how much have you learned about Islam?"

"I know that Jesus is not God or the Son of God."

"If you know this, then you must have some proof to back up this belief system that has brought you to that conclusion."

"Well, I read it in that book, *What Did Jesus Really Say?* When we get back inside the cell, I'll tell you my proofs, which can be found in the Bible, as clear as day."

"What else is it that you can tell me you have learned?"

"I learned that the Prophet David, who was a King, KingDawud, asked Allah what was the least that he has blessed us with? Allah told him to breathe in. That is amazing because I was never thankful for the air feeling as if it was something owed to me. So many people suffer from lung diseases and other ailments which make it hard for them even to take a breath each day.

"I've also learned that we are in no position to question our Lord because we are not wise enough to do so, and neither do we have the authority to question him."

Kent paused, then said,

"I read a story in the Quran's footnotes, where Musa (Moses), who had considered himself to be the wisest man on earth, was told by Allah that he wasn't at all the wisest man on earth. He was sent on a journey by Allah to find the man named Khidr, who was much wiser than himself.

"When Musa found Khidr, he told him he wanted to travel with him so he might be able to acquire some of the knowledge that he had. Khidr told him, 'You will not be able to find yourself patient with me. How can you find yourself patient with that which you do not at all understand?'

"Musa said, 'If you allow me to travel with you, I will not ask you questions, and you will find me one of those who is patient.'

"This being said, Khidr agreed to allow Musa to travel with him. They got into a boat and while at the back of the boat, where no one could see him do it, Khidr took a sharp nail and knocked a hole in the boat. When Musa saw this, he got very angry, saying to Khidr, 'Why have you sabotaged these people's boat when they have been generous enough to give you and me a free ride?' Khidr turned to Musa and said, 'Didn't I tell you that you would not be able to find yourself being patient with me?' Musa said, 'Forgive me, for if I forget, I will not ask you any more questions.'

"Once they got off the boat and had traveled a ways away from the sea, they encountered a group of small, innocent children playing in an open field. Khidr walked up to one of the little boys

171

and cut his throat, killing him. Musa was enraged. He ran to Khidr and said, 'How wicked of a man are you to murder an innocent child that has not done a thing to anyone at all?' Again, Khidr turned to him and said, 'Didn't I tell you that you would never be able to find patience with me?'

"Musa said, as he followed behind Khidr, 'Forgive me for forgetting, and if I question you again, then you are entitled to remove me from your presence.'

"For a long time, the two of them traveled by foot, and when they had gone days without food or water, they went to the door of a house they found to ask for food. The people inside refused to help them at all. As Musa stood there, trying to convince them to aid him and Khidr, he turned around to find Khidr rebuilding and fixing the wooden gate that had fallen around the house, until it looked like new.

"Musa ran to Khidr and yelled, 'How dare you fix up this gate of theirs when they have refused us food and shelter? Had you chosen to then, you could have demanded a price for this.' Khidr stopped what he was doing and turned to face Musa. He said, 'This is the point where you and I depart from each other's company. Before I leave you, I will tell you why I did the things you've seen me do that with which you were unable to have patience.

"'The boat we rode on was being pursued by a tyrant king who was not far from catching up to it and stopping it by force. When he did reach the ship, all he saw were the people, soaking wet, on the bank, instead. That prompted the king to go down the river. The people's only source of income was their boat and had they ceased using it, they would have starved, so I placed a hole in it so that the king would not see it when he passed. By day, the people will have swum to the bottom, where the boat is, and pulled it back up to land, where they will fix it. This way, they will have their means of support again.

"'As for the child, his parents, who were rulers over that land, had done many bad things against their Lord. In return for their disobedience, the Lord had given them an heir who would destroy everything they had built, leaving their legacy in ruins. The parents repented for what they did, so Allah took away his curse, and they are now going to have a son who will be righteous and just.

"'As for this gate you see me placing back in its rightful place, a man who was righteous has two children living in that home. He begged Allah to protect their wealth that he placed under the ground, so only they would receive it. The next time that gate falls, the man's two sons will be strong enough to rebuild it, and they will find the inheritance that Allah intended for them to have.'"

Chapter 25

From the back door where he stood, Tawheed smiled and looked at his beautiful wife; she and his daughter sat on the couch in the living room, reviewing Arabic words. Seeing her father, ShuQuran ran to him,

"Daddy!"

He smiled and scooped her up in his arms.

"*Salaamu Alaikim*, his wife said, going to him and smiling as he reached out to her.

He embraced her with a kiss, still feeling as if he was dreaming and, somehow, she wasn't even real.

"Why do you look at me like that every time you see me," she asked, smiling.

"You seem too good to be true, so I am still getting used to living in this wonderful dream, with what is a true blessing from Allah."

She smiled at his words, but he knew something was bothering her from her body language. He set his daughter down and said,

"ShuQuran, go play so I can talk to Tawheeda."

"Okay, Dad," she said, turning back to smile at him before she started to run.

"Tawheeda, something is bothering you. I only hope you are not displeased with me as your husband because I am trying as hard as I can to be the best husband and provider I am capable of being."

She clasped his face in her hands and smiled,

"You are the best thing that has ever happened to me. If I have any complaints, then you should know that it is not due to what you and I have."

"So what is bothering you," he asked.

He took her hand and led her outside to their large wooden patio at the back of their house. She looked into his eyes and said,

"What do you think of my best friend?"

"Who, Safa?"

"Yes, Safa," she said, beginning to wipe tears from her eyes.

"Did something happen to Safa," Tawheed asked, with concern in his voice.

"I just found out from her that a few months ago she went to some club looking for two of her friends, and some man got her drunk, then raped her on the floor of the club. I can't believe she didn't tell me," Tawheeda said, looking at her husband, who was speechless.

"Did she get treated to see if his sperm was left inside of her so that the police can identify the rapist?"

"I don't want you to kill the man who did this, Tawheed, and no, she didn't go to the police because if she had, then everyone would know she got raped, which means they would also know that she is no longer a virgin. If they know she is no longer a virgin, then no one will be willing to marry her, especially because she didn't lose her virginity while married."

"I'm so sorry that she is going through this, but if she is not willing to go to the police and she has no idea of who the rapist was, how can I do anything to help her?"

Tawheeda looked deeply into his eyes, as tears rushed down her cheeks. He wiped them away with his fingers. Finally, Tawheeda stared into his eyes and said,

"Marry her."

"Marry her?"

Tawheed was puzzled by what she said.

"Yes, marry her. I want for you to marry her."

"It will not bother you to share me with another woman?"

"We, as Muslims, want for our sisters and brothers that which we want for ourselves and she is like a baby sister to me, so I want for her to be as happy as I am. I want you to make her as happy as you have made me."

"If it will make you happy, I'll marry her," Tawheed said, looking into Tawheeda's tear-filled eyes.

Then he embraced her. He greatly admired Safa, but he hoped his choice to marry her would not put a strain on the relationship that he and Tawheeda had established.

Chapter 26

From where he sat, on the top bunk, Kent peered down at the Sheikh as he offered his last prayer of the day to Allah. When he finished, he stood, then walked to the toilet, where he sat, facing forward. He then began to relieve himself, which made Kent laugh. After he finished relieving himself, the Sheikh rinsed himself with water, then got up from the toilet. He turned on the water in the sink and began performing *wudu*.

When he turned around, Kent looked at him and asked,

"Why do you always sit down, or kneel, when you use the toilet? I was always taught that was something only females done."

"You were probably also taught that only females shaved the private area between their legs and shaved the hair from under their armpits, right?"

"Yeah, I noticed you do that too, so what's going on?"

"Well, after I answer your questions, you will give me the proof of the things I asked you about earlier, correct?"

"Yeah, I'll do that."

"Okay then," the Sheikh said, before sitting on his bed.

"Whenever you stand up to urinate, the pressure from your urine hits the toilet water, and it sprays back up onto your legs. You are unable to see it, but urine flies all over you. If you urinate even once a day, you have a lot of urine all over your body and clothes. So can you imagine how filthy people are at the end of the day,

183

when they stand up and urinate, especially if they have stood to urinate more than this?

"Next time you use the toilet standing, do yourself a favor and stand with your boxers or your shorts on; you'll feel the urine as it jumps back up onto your legs."

The Sheikh continued explaining to Kent,

"Also, you will notice that we, or I, use a bottle of water to rinse myself off every time I relieve myself. Toilet tissue is not sufficient to clean urine or feces from the human body. It's just like if a person has dirt or blood on them. They don't just wipe it away and expect their garment or skin to be clean. They use water and soap, but most people who are not Muslim, don't even care if urine is all over them."

Kent began to wonder how much urine he had all over his body, after urinating more than twelve times throughout the day. He said,

"I never thought about it like that."

The Sheikh continued,

"I'm sure you have dealt with a woman on the streets when you were out there. Am I right?"

"Yeah, you're right, but what does that have to do with this conversation about pissing?"

"When you would go to those women, wouldn't you make sure that you had on clean clothes and clean underwear?"

"Of course. It would be embarrassing to pull your pants down in front of a woman, just to have urine stains in your drawers."

"We, as men, beautify ourselves for a woman. We men get on our knees to propose to them, and we get on our knees to pleasure them while making love to them, but man has a problem with getting on his knees to worship the one who has created her and him

"What I am telling you is, if a man is going to beautify himself, to go before a woman who does not deserve a special honor over the Lord of us all, then why would I go to him in prayers with filth all over myself and my garments?"

"That makes sense," Kent said.

The Sheikh continued explaining,

"As for the hair under the armpits and in the pubic area, it serves absolutely no purpose. When a man sweats, the sweat and dirt run down his body, resting in this area. When we wipe ourselves, we push the feces into the pores of the hairs in that area. Our hair has pores, in case you didn't know, and that is why you often see, even after you have cleaned yourself thoroughly, there is a dirty residue on your white boxers. It comes from the dirt and feces that is inside the pores of your hairs.

"A lot of dirt gathers under our armpits, and even when we wash the hair, we are unable to get to the skin beneath, so the area is still filthy. That is the reason for removing the hair from those two places. Since we all know women do it, based on how clean they are, then you should never be ashamed to imitate them in their cleanliness."

The Sheikh changed topics, remembering what Kent was to tell him.

"Now, as for you, what are the proofs of the things you told me you learned earlier? Knowledge is to comprehend a thing as it is with certainty."

Kent reached under his bed, trying to grab the book he had been studying, but then he stopped. He looked at the doctor and said,

"In Matthew 7:21, Jesus says, 'not everyone that sayeth to me, Jesus Lord, Lord, shall we enter into the kingdom of heaven, but that doeth the will of my Father which is in heaven.'

"The scholars of Islam have said that this means that the term, father, is used for God in numerous places in the Bible, but it is never used exclusively for Jesus, and this shows one that Jesus is not the divine God. Even if he was called upon as Lord, he could not admit anyone into Paradise.

"Again, in Matthew 11:15, Jesus says, 'I thank you, Father, Lord of the heavens and earth because thou hast hid these things from the wise and prudent and has revealed them unto babes.'

"Again, this is showing that Jesus is submitting to a higher power than himself, meaning that he is not God. In Matthew 14:23, Jesus says, 'And when he had sent the multitudes away, he went up into a mountain apart to pray.' The scholars have said if Jesus is God or a part of God, then why does he pray? In fact, prayer is always from a submitting, needy and dependent one, for the mercy of Almighty Allah."

"In Matthew 15:22-28," Kent continued," it reads, and a woman of Canaan came out of the same coast and cried unto him, saying have mercy on me, o Lord, thou son of David; My daughter is grievously vexed with a devil, but he answered her not a word, and his disciples came and besought him, saying send her away, for she crieth after us. But he answered and said, I am but sent unto the lost sheep of the house of Israel.

'Then she came and worshiped him, saying Lord help me, but he answered and said, it is not meet to take the children's bread and cast it to dogs, and she said truth Lord, yet dogs eat of the crumbs which fall from the master's table.'

"This shows the lack of love and mercy on Jesus' part; he degraded a woman, calling her a dog, and he uplifted his tribe and not others; he tells them he was not sent to care for or deliver them from ruin. A woman who is ignorant debated with him, convincing him of other than he had originally agreed to.

"This shows that Jesus was sent to a specific group of people and not everyone, as people believe he was, and he says that in his own words."

Kent was becoming surer of his studies and what they meant. He went on,

"In Matthew 19:16-17, it says, behold, one came after and said unto him, Good Master, what good thing shall I do today that I may have life eternal? And he said unto him, why callest thou me good, for there is no good but one god.

"This is a clear indication that he is separating himself from God and giving no glory to himself or divinity to himself as the Christians of today give him. If he didn't place himself on this pedestal, then those people outside of him, who are less than him, have no right to do so.

"Again, in Matthew 21:45-46, it states that the chief priests and Pharisees perceived that he spoke of them, but when they sought to lay hands on him, they feared the multitude because they took him for a prophet.

The next lesson Kent had completed left him with questions. He said,

"The priests and Pharisees are still today considered to be the wisest among the Christians, as they were in the time of Jesus and these wise men took Jesus as a prophet not the son of God or a part of God, so why now have people begun taking him as God or part of god?"

The Sheikh, who had been listening and thinking, said,

"Good question. You will see in the *Merriam-Webster Encyclopedia of World Religions*, which is in the library, that the ruler Constantine, who was considered a Roman god, assembled and ran the Council of Nicea, and there is when Jesus' status was raised from a man to a god."

Kent replied, continuing to tell the Sheikh what he had learned,

"I have also read in the Bible that Jesus preached about the one god you Muslims worship, who is the same god that Moses or Abraham worshiped. I also have noticed that Moses of Abraham never told their people to worship Jesus, but they always preached for them to worship this one true god," Kent said, stating,

"In the Bible, this is made clear in Matthew 12:28-30, where Jesus was asked by a scribe, which is the first commandment of all. He answered by saying the first commandment of all the commandments is hear o Israel, the Lord thy god is one Lord; and thou shall love the Lord thy god with all thy heart and with all thy soul; and with all of thy mind and with all of thy strength; this is the first commandment.

"There is only one God, not two, not three but one. Now as for Jesus speaking and prophesying about the prophet Muhammad to come after him, it is in John 14:15-16; John 15:26-27; John 16:5-88; John 16:12-14; and John 16:16. In all these verses, Jesus prophesied that he must leave so that a comforter will come after him to teach the people what it is that he has not yet taught them.

"My question to you is this, If Jesus was a god or a part of God or his son, then who in the world or the heavens can teach a man more than he was unable to teach them? And if he is God's son, how could someone be able to come after him to do that which he was unable to do?"

The Sheikh replied,

"You just answered your own question. Whenever someone comes after you, then that means they will be held accountable to do that which you were not capable of doing, or they have come to complete that which you were unable to complete.

"Christians believe that the one he is talking about to come after him is the Holy Spirit."

Kent listened carefully, but then he asked,

"Well if God the Father, the Son and the Holy Spirit are one and Jesus was in the constant company of the Holy Spirit, why would he need to leave so that which has been with him the whole time can come?"

The Sheikh smiled at the question, knowing that Kent was able to see through contradictions. He said,

190

"Even if this being or thing that was to come after was a ghost, do you think anyone would stand around and listen to a ghost? Or if they did have the courage to do so, do you think, if they told someone else that a ghost has been informing them about things, that they will not be considered crazy? And whatever it was they said would be considered frivolous?

"Allah has sent men to talk to men since the beginning of time, so why now would he send a ghost which will scare the souls out of men to talk to them?

"We as Muslims realize that Muhammad, who was a man, was sent as Allah's final prophet and messenger and if the Christians would study their own books, like the Gospel of Barnabas, which is in the Library of Congress, they too would see the truth of this."

The lesson was over, but the Sheikh said to Kent,

"You did well, and I am proud of you, but if you will excuse me, I must study the information about my case."

He pulled a manila folder from under his bunk; he had studied the contents every night.

Kent wanted to ask him why he had a life sentence or what it was that he was studying, but he figured his questions about that would eventually be answered, as well.

Chapter 27

Being one who knew the *Sunna* (legal way) of the Prophet Muhammad (whom may peace be upon) did not stop Tawheed from going into a jewelry store in a Georgetown shopping center to buy his soon-to-be new bride, Safa, the customary jewelry a woman usually received the day of the wedding.

As he walked to the male clerk standing behind the counter, reading a GQ magazine while listening to loud music, Tawheed's palms began to sweat.

He didn't want to be ridiculed for trying to buy over thirty-thousand dollars' worth of jewelry, when it was well-known that the Prophet of Islam told a man that marriage was half of his religion, and he should get married as soon as he was able, or he should fast.

The Prophet said that even if a man had no wealth except for an iron ring, he should give this to his bride, or if he didn't have that much, then he should recite to her what he had memorized of the Quran.

"What's up homie," the clerk asked with a smile. "You interested in that ring and necklace right there, right?"

He was a Middle Eastern-looking man, whose hair was curly. The speech of the man had thrown Tawheed off for a second, but he was sure that he was Muslim, so instead of saying what's up, he greeted him by saying,

"*Salaamu Alaikum.*"

"*Wa Alaikum salaamu Ahki,*" the clerk said.

He came from behind the counter to where Tawheed stood and said,

"Whenever you see what you want, tell me, and I'll give you, my Muslim brother discount, alright?"

Tawheed nodded his head and continued looking in the glass jewelry case in front of him. There were so many beautiful pieces of jewelry that he could barely decide which of them he intended to purchase. He thought about his first wife, Tawheeda, which brought a smile to his face. He pondered whether she would be jealous if he brought Safa some jewelry that was more expensive than the jewelry he had brought her the day of their wedding.

Tawheeda loved Safa very much, and he had yet to see any signs of jealousy between them, but he knew that a woman still had a certain amount of jealousy in her heart when it came to her man.

The clerk interrupted his thoughts. He revealed the huge diamond necklace that he had placed around his own neck and said,

"You buy her something like this, and you'll have her in bed every night and all day."

Tawheed turned to face the clerk and asked,

196

"Where you from?"

"Yemen."

"Yemen?"

"Yes."

Tawheed said,

"Yemen, that's like a really strict Muslim country, if I'm not mistaken."

"Yeah, they're too Islamic, and that's why I had to leave the place. It's no fun to be had in Yemen, and for a playboy like me, who has hundreds of beautiful ladies, I can't be stuck in Yemen where everyone else wants to pray all day and the ladies can't be yours unless you marry them."

"That's interesting to hear you say," Tawheed replied. "I always looked up to you Arab brothers, thinking ya'll possess the Islam knowledge in manner and application. Are you even married?"

"Yeah, I'm married, of course. I got married when I was thirteen," the clerk said.

He approached Tawheed and took his wallet from his pocket. He opened it and pulled out a picture of his wife and two kids. Tawheed was shocked at how beautiful the wife was that he had to lower his gaze. He asked,

"So when was the last time you saw your wife and children?"

"It's been like four or five years; I'm busy with the six businesses I got here in the States, so I rarely have the time to go to Yemen. Besides, I have another wife and like twenty concubines here to keep me busy."

Tawheed just shook his head, disgusted at what the brother had just said.

"So can't she divorce you for the abandonment of her and your kids?"

"Yeah, right. You don't know anything about Arab women, I see. Her entire family will disown her if she even thought about divorcing me and no man in our country will be looking to marry her, knowing that she couldn't wait for her husband to return."

"You have the ability to go visit, but you're not even trying to go see them, and that's the difference."

"There is no difference. I had her since she was ten years old, so I've grown tired of her. Besides, many of us marry our cousins; that way, even if she wants to leave, she'll never be able to go far, because she's still in the family."

"Man, ya'll worse than how my homies, who ping women or just play them out. Ya'll real cold-hearted brothers, when it comes to the sisters. And what's up with all this jewelry you're wearing? It's *haram* for a man to wear gold."

The brother looked down at his bracelet, watch and chain and smiled. He looked back up at Tawheed and said,

198

"I'm Esam Al Mansory, the fly-est Arab on the face of the earth. All these beautiful freaky women here in the States love this shiny stuff."

"How can you be fornicating when it is haram to do so? Actually, you're committing adultery, which is a crime punishable by death in Islam."

"Hey, if you wanna live an Islamic life, then be my guest and go ahead, but many people in Muslim countries wish they could come to America to do the things many of the Islamic countries do not allow them to do."

"Like use women for their bodies, right?"

"You have never used women for their bodies?"

"To be honest, I have always wanted to get married because when you sleep with a lot of women that you have no feelings for, it will quench your sexual desire, but you'll never be happy or feel complete with them."

"Man, you're freakin' crazy," Esam said.

He went back behind the counter near the cash register. He asked,

"You don't see how most Arab men come here and take over this place in no time? We own all the gas stations, the shops inside of the malls, the restaurants, and more. Your people just sell drugs and pimp women, so how can you even try to look down on anyone else?"

"First of all, those men are not my people. The Muslims are my people. Secondly, you brag about the stores and things that you brothers have but all the restaurants that ya'll own sell liquor, which is *haram*. The gas stations ya'll own sell cigarettes, condoms, and many more *haram* things.

"Did you come here to do more bad than good? If so, then you're only bringing yourself closer to the hellfire. It seems that you have given up the truth for disbelief and I know now why the Prophet said there will be a people who are on the brink of the Paradise, but they will be turned back from it and that there are people from the hellfire who will come a footstep away from it but will be turned back of being admitted to Paradise."

"Get out of my store! I don't wanna hear no more of this junk," Esam said, getting angry.

Tawheed walked back across the store and exited immediately. He began to think about something he had heard Morpheus say to Neo, in The Matrix, 'There was a difference between knowing the truth and living the truth.'

Chapter 28

Kent was doing push-ups in the cell with his shirt off. As the Sheikh entered, Kent asked him,

"So how was your visit?"

"It was a very good visit. I received some good information and some information you would call not so good. And by the way, cover your belly button, because if what is between your navel and to below your knees is not covered, then you are considered naked."

Kent stopped working out long enough to put his shirt back on. He looked at the Sheikh, who was busy looking through the manila folder. He had busied himself with that folder for the four years they had been in the cell together. Kent asked,

"So are you gonna tell me about the good and not-so-good news that you got while in the visiting hall?"

The Sheikh closed the folder and looked at him.

"Well, young man, today my lawyer came here to see me, and he told me that the charges I am here for were over-turned by the appeals court."

"That's great! That means you're gonna beat me home," Kent said, smiling.

"Well, then there's the not-so-good news. Originally, I was charged with another crime, and they have re-indicted me for this crime, so I'm not going home next month along with you," the Sheikh said, smiling back.

"Man, that's messed up! This government is so wicked. All the crimes we do are not even a dot, compared to the ones they are doing on a daily basis. This is the United States of America we live in!"

"Calm down. It is Allah's decree that I am here and no matter how much I don't like it, I can't push it back, so I am satisfied with what it is that my Lord has chosen to test me with."

"So what is it they say you did that is preventing them from letting you go?"

The Sheikh looked at the ground, ashamed to even mention the crime he had been charged with. He looked up again, into Kent's eyes and said,

"I was charged with raping and killing a woman that I never saw before in my life. She was on the part of the bike trail off Four Mile Run in Arlington, Virginia, where I have a home with my wife.

"I was making love to my wife when I heard the woman screaming. Without thinking about it, I jumped up, got dressed and ran out of the house to save her.

"The same officers who tried to get me for a charge of terrorism showed up to arrest me for that crime."

Hearing what the Sheikh said sent chills through Kent's body. He stood there, speechless, with a distant look on his face.

"Are you okay," the Sheikh asked, looking at Kent with a disturbed expression.

Without answering, Kent left the cell. He couldn't believe what he had just heard.

Here was a man, sitting in jail for the rest of his life, for a crime that he himself had committed! He knew he had to do something; he had to make right the wrong he had committed on that woman. But with less than ten days left on his sentence, he wasn't willing to do a life sentence. No man would be.

Chapter 29

And the *mu azzin* (caller to prayer) stood and began calling the *Athan* (call to prayer); Doctor Tamimi looked around the gymnasium at the brothers who had gathered on the floor for *ju mah salaah* (Friday prayer). He was hoping to see Kent, who had renamed himself Qareem, but he had yet to show. After taking his *shahada* over two years ago, Kent, who was in love with his new way of life, hadn't missed one week of *ju mah salaah*. That caused the Sheikh to worry.

From a distance, Qareem watched as the last brother entered the gym. He knew that in the morning he would be a free man. The excitement of going back to the world as a much better man made him feel better than he had ever felt in his life. He knew he had committed a lot of wrongs, but that Kent no longer existed; he was Qareem, a new man.

He sat there in a daze. He thought about the Sheikh and the other men he would be leaving behind who had to remain in prison for the rest of their lives. He felt bad, knowing if he had to do the time they were doing, he wouldn't be able to handle it.

He then began thinking about something the Sheikh had told him about Allah allowing for a man to spend the rest of his life in prison.

The Sheikh had said it was a mercy to the man and others from Allah, being that the people of the world were now free of his treachery and barbaric ways. He also was free from the temptations for committing wrong, which gave him a better chance to enter Paradise.

The men in prison were more than likely to obtain Paradise because the worldly distractions had been cleared from their paths and the things which tempted them the most were out of their reach.

A tear fell from his eye, and he went down the hallway and headed for the block. He picked up the phone to call his lawyer. When he finished talking, he could feel a cold chill all over his body.

At the same time, he felt as free as he had ever felt the entire time he had been alive.

He went to the gym, entering through the front door. Seeing him, the Sheikh, who had grown very fond of him, smiled. Just as the Imam was about to deliver the *khutbah* (religious sermon), a message came over the loud speaker, ordering Doctor Tamimi to come to R and D and be immediately released.

The Sheikh looked at Kent with a confused expression on his face.
        "Alhamdu lillah, Sheikh, they are calling for you to be released immediately," the Imam said, with a smile on his face.

The Sheikh, who couldn't believe what he was hearing, began to cry. Kent hugged him then said,

"No man shall bear the burden of another man, either in this life or the next."

The End

Kingdawud Mujahid Burgess

Kingdawud Mujahid Burgess continues to deliver a wide variety of content; spanning from real life street stories engulfed in the criminal mindset. Turning the page, Kingdawud, shows you the battle of man dealing with his existence and spirituality, the code of the street is not the only rules a man will abide by. He shows how these men are tested by the street and their faith. This is his third published book with more to come.

www.ingramcontent.com/pod-product-compliance
Lightning Source LLC
Chambersburg PA
CBHW030320020726
47493CB00004B/1102